Annabeth's War

Annabeth's War

By Jessica Greyson

Ready Writer Press

Annabeth's War

Published by: Ready Writer Press
Cover Design by Louie Roybal III
www.louieroybal.com

ISBN: 978-0-9884614-6-8 (hardcover)

DEDICATION

This book is lovingly dedicated to the One who has taught me that everything is beautiful in His time.

To Lily, my twin in heart, best friend, and sister in spirit. Your friendship and encouragement made this possible.

Thank you for helping me touch the stars.

CONTENTS

Prologue

Annabeth took a deep breath looking up at the five tall boys before her. Curling her fingers, she rubbed them against her palms, wishing she held a sword in her hand. As the first boy stepped forward, Annabeth's eyes fell to the ground. She was biting the inside of her cheek and wriggling her toes in her shoes. Her heart wished that she had begged her father to take her with him to see Lord Raburn, but she didn't like Lord Raburn. He had a way of making her uncomfortable and getting her to say all kinds of things she never meant to say. He had, ever since she was little. She just couldn't keep her mouth shut around that man.

"What do you think you are doing here?" asked the tall boy, his body language saying he was ready for a fight.

"Going for a walk. I want to pick some flowers."

"Going for a walk?"

"Pick flowers!" interjected a second boy, stepping forward.

"Yes," she answered quietly. *A soft answer turns away wrath*; she heard her mother's voice in the back of her mind. It had been three years since her mother's passing, and that voice seemed to come less to her mind. While most girls her age were learning how to mend clothes and bake bread, she was learning to...a blush crept up her neck. *Swordfight.* Her father's ceaseless instruction and pointers were constantly running through her brain. Maybe that is why her mother's words came less and less. At least her father hadn't sent her away from him.

"I didn't think girls *like you* could pick flowers."

"I like to pick flowers," she said quietly, hoping they would just leave her alone.

The boy scoffed. "Yeah, right." His hand flew across her face, spinning her dizzily to the ground.

"Aren't so good without a sword, are you?"

Her head reeled. She didn't answer as she placed her cold hand against her burning cheek.

"What? Too stupid to answer?"

The second boy jerked her braid. She winced. "Answer him, midget."

"What was that for?" she asked instead of answered.

With swiftness she was jerked to her feet.

"What was that for? You idiot! Don't you dare beat me in a sword fight again," he said, throwing her bodily away. She crashed into another, who grabbed her hair to help her stand up and shook her as he hissed.

"Or me, it's plain embarrassing." He shoved her away to another until each had whispered his hate for her and then tossed her to the ground between the five of them.

"Promise that you won't."

Her heart was racing. She couldn't promise. If her father wanted her to do it—if her father wanted her to train with the boys he was teaching, she'd get in more trouble for not beating them, and her already grueling training could become more so.

There was a kick to her ribs.

"Promise."

Annabeth set her lips together, blinking back the tears that came to her eyes.

"I have do to what my father tells me."

"Well, it won't mean beating us. Not if we can help it."

Annabeth pulled into a tight ball, her arms protecting her head and face as five of her father's students seemed to pile on her all at once.

There was a voice from above and the load lightened as various howls were given above her.

"Off with all of you! You should be ashamed of yourself, you cowards!" shouted the voice as the last one scampered off.

For a moment she wished that whoever was standing above her would simply walk away and let her get up and drag herself home as she tried not to cry. Only weak people cried. She couldn't be weak. But no, whoever it was knelt beside her.

"Are you okay?"

Slowly Annabeth uncurled to look at the face

above hers. Shock ripped through her.

"Your highness," she murmured dropping her gaze.

"You're the sword master's daughter, aren't you." It was more a statement than a question.

Annabeth nodded. It was beyond her why *he,* Prince Alfred, would wish to speak to her. She was a nobody, a commoner, the daughter of a soldier—a gifted soldier, a master of the sword.

"Do you think you can stand up?" he asked.

"I am sure I can," she said, pushing herself from the ground.

His eyes ran over her. "Are you sure you are okay?"

Annabeth glanced at her dress. It was soiled and torn. "Nothing that time and little soap and water won't mend."

"You have a scratch on your cheek."

Annabeth touched her face to find the cut, and winced. A sharp stone must have cut her in all the fighting despite her attempt to protect herself.

"You should let your mother look at that," said Prince Alfred softly.

"I don't have a mother, your highness."

Pain flashed through his eyes, "Neither do I," the Prince murmured, and Annabeth wished she had held her tongue. The loss of the queen had been heavy on the king and the kingdom.

"Is your father away?"

Annabeth just nodded, not wishing to say anything that would cause the prince pain.

"Then you should come up to the castle to have it tended."

Annabeth shook her head, "You are too kind, your highness. I am just a commoner; I can't come in."

"You haven't come into the castle?"

"No, just the courtyard with my father for training."

Prince Alf's eyes widened. "Well, you should come and get that tended to."

"But I am too dirty."

"Don't you mind that; my grandmother can take care of you."

"Thank you, your highness, but no," and dropping her best curtsy she stepped away from him and turned her homeward way

.

CHAPTER 1

The small town was bursting at the seams; it was a country holiday, and everyone that could be there was in attendance. Traveling troupes, jugglers, tumblers, and puppeteers all drew large throngs of commoners, but the crowd was exceptionally large around a tall man with honest blue eyes and brown hair.

He had a charming smile that disarmed any fear of the silvery blade in his hand as it whistled and sang, glittering skillfully with his every move. He was daring anyone to fight him for the chance to win a prize.

The jingling bag of coins often caught men's eyes more readily then the blade he wielded. For a few coppers or a piece of silver, they could try their chances with him—a duel of pure skill for a bag full of money.

A small youth with a green cap pulled almost over his eyes pressed his way to the front of the group, breathing heavily. He caught the tail end of the fight, his eyes carefully flitting over the faces in the crowd.

"Who will fight me? Surely there must be another man among you who is willing to try his mettle with me. Strong, brave, manly. Yes, you take a chance of losing that pretty piece of silver, but look at the bounty you could gain," said the man, jingling the bag of coins as incentive.

Almost reluctantly, a man stepped forward. "I'll fight you," he said, flipping his coin towards the man.

The swordsman caught it with his free hand. His charming smile making another appearance, he dropped the coin into the bag, where it made a most satisfactory sound. "Very good, sir."

The fight was short, for though the man had strength enough to hew down a small tree with a single blow, he had little cunning compared to the swordsman.

"Well done, sir. Should there ever be a battle, I would like to know you are on my side."

The man turned away, grumbling, and disappeared into the crowd.

"Anyone else care to take a chance? Four men bested seems like a lot, but who knows—there might be someone better than I hiding in this crowd. We never know when we may meet our better. Are you hiding in the crowd ready to set my world upside down?"

The crowd glanced around hesitatingly; people began to disperse.

"Well, anyone?"

The youth curled his sweating palms into fists and then released them, pulling a single silver coin from a seemingly empty pouch that hung limp at his belt. He glanced around again, swallowing a lump in his throat.

The coin bag jingled fair with promises. "Come, you all can't be tired of such entertainment. Think, sir, what would your fair lady say if you fought with me?"

"Mine would say I was a fool," uttered the man from the depths of the crowd.

"I am not so sure about that, sir. It is not every day you get such a chance as I am offering you," he said, jingling the bag of coins again.

The man turned and disappeared. The crowd was thinning quickly now; a few hopeful onlookers stayed, wishing for one more fight with the swordsman and his glorious blade that never seemed to fail.

The youth turned the coin over in his hand again, glancing nervously around.

"Last chance. If someone doesn't speak up now, I shall leave. A perfect chance gone forever." He passed the youth and continued around. He had nearly completed the full circle that would end his offer of wealth...when a voice suddenly spoke up.

"I'll fight you, since everyone else seems afraid to," the youth said, stepping forward.

The crowd laughed and the swordsman turned around. His eyebrows rose. "I am sorry, but I do believe that you are a little undercut."

"My coin is as good as anyone else's," he said, flashing the coin in his hand.

"You are barely old enough to be wielding such a sword."

"I know, but I am willing to take the challenge."

"You are a lad. A mere sapling."

"Well, since you are such a tall tree, maybe a wind will come and blow you over."

The crowd laughed.

"If you are certain you want to part with that silver coin, lad…"

"How do you know you won't be parting with yours?"

"The day that happens due to youth such as yourself, the world will have come to an end."

"Well, maybe it's my lucky day. Then I won't need your coin; I'll be walking on streets of gold."

"You better watch your tongue, lad. You might be singing with the angels sooner than you think," said the swordsman, swinging his blade back and forth, causing the air to whistle as he cut it.

"It is a risk I am willing to take, but let's stop

sharpening our tongues on each other. Will you take my coin or no?"

"If it is as good as you say."

"Better," he said with an awkward toss.

The swordsman snatched it from the air and tossed it into his bag without looking. It made a pleasant sound as it landed among the others.

The youth wiped his sweaty hands on his doublet before withdrawing his sword.

The swordsman's eyes narrowed. *What kind of lad would let the world know he is that nervous?*

The youth reacquainted himself with the feel of his sword with a few ready swings and took his stance.

"Are you sure you are ready? We could wait until you grow up, you know," said the swordsman, looking over his small opponent.

"We could, but someone else might have bested you by then."

"Well, I always like to know whom I have the honor of fighting. What is your name?"

The boy hesitated a moment before answering. "Bartholomew."

"It's a pleasure, Bartholomew, and I am Ransom. Are you ready?"

The youth nodded, his hat bobbing.

"You get the first chance to strike then," said Ransom with a nod as he opened himself up for the youth's attack.

The first blow against Ransom's sword was hesitant, soft, almost afraid. He glanced it off and held ready for a second, his stance inviting another strike. It came stronger this time and he deflected, letting it sing against the length of his blade.

Then the fight began in earnest. Ransom took his time mounting his hardened skills against the youth. The fight warmed up as Bartholomew's skill showed. Their swords locked. Ransom looked into the boy's eyes. They were earnest and intent on their swords. Desperation showed in the lad's blue eyes. But was it really a he? Now so close, Ransom took a moment to study the youth intently. Smooth skin, clean hands, and face, the hair so completely concealed beneath the hat, the soft pleasant scent seemed to hover about...was it a she?

Instead of bringing the lock to a crisis, Bartholomew spun away. The next blow caught neatly against his sword.

All right; time to heat things up. You have had

your fun, now for mine. Ransom's blade flew through the air. It was matched blow for blow. Bartholomew's skill surprised him, and in a momentary pause, he looked again into the youth's eyes. There was an intensity-desire-need-hunger—and desperation—lurking there.

They were eyes that reminded him of his own haunted youth. His heart lurched.

He'll have to learn the hard way. Then, the youth's spin away from him ran through his brain. It was a dance-like spin, the spin of a girl in a new dress. *No…if this is who I am looking for…she is the one.*

Time to raise the stakes. How much do you really know, and how much is left in your purse?

The swords began to sing as they clashed hard, strong, and frequently. In a close-range battle, Ransom severed the purse from the youth's belt. It fell to the ground.

Empty. So that is why you so desperately wagered your last piece of silver for a chance at a small fortune. Time to bring this to a close.

He made his move. It should have flung the sword into the air and right into his hand, but the youth saw it coming and tried to recoil from the blow. The sword left Bartholomew's hands and clattered on the cobblestones. They both lunged for it, but Bartholomew was there first. A headlong dash brought it into his grasp and, still on the ground; he whirled around, holding off the sword that was nearly at his throat. He tumbled away, rolling to his feet, blade meeting blade. As he stood, they locked swords.

Bartholomew's eyes flickered around the crowd. His face paled for a moment, a flash of recognition flitting through his blue eyes. "This needs to be over," he murmured.

Pushing away from the lock, Bartholomew's onslaught against Ransom was sudden and full.

All right; let's see how you handle this, thought Ransom, loosening the grip on his sword. The swords flew from their hands as he struck Bartholomew's. They clattered to the feet of the onlookers.

The crowd was thick. They were all holding their breath, waiting for what would happen next—ready and waiting to cheer. But who was the winner? The man? The boy? Both? Neither? Would they run for their swords and resume the fight?

Bartholomew stood, waiting for Ransom's cue.

"Can you wrestle as well as you fight?" Ransom asked.

"No, sir," said Bartholomew, taking a step back.

Ransom's face broke into a smile and he bowed slightly at the waist. "Well, call it a draw—for a later time."

The crowd broke into a cheer. Bartholomew turned, shying away as he retrieved his sword.

Any other boy would be beaming ear to ear, eating up the praise and encouraging it, thought Ransom. He stepped towards the youth. "Well, I bested you, so that makes me the winner, and you bested me, so that makes you the winner. So, shall we split the spoils?"

"Sounds fair to me," said Bartholomew, retrieving his purse from where it had fallen. "Did you really have to do this?" he asked, picking it up.

"Unfortunate casualty," said Ransom with a shrug. He offered the youth a handful of coins from his own bag.

"Thank you," Bartholomew said with a slight bow, and started making his way into the crowd.

"Won't you join me?" asked Ransom, laying his hand on the youth's shoulder.

"Join you?" Bartholomew asked, shrugging off Ransom's hand and putting distance between them.

"Two swordsmen are better than one. It is a good way to earn a livelihood," he said with a shake of his coin sack.

"Good for one person, but not two. Good day." With that, he turned to lose himself in the crowd.

Taking his time, Ransom followed the boy as he mingled in and out of the crowd, changing directions several times. The boy seemed relaxed; he would have melted into the mass, if no one had been looking, but people were watching him.

Bartholomew was flushing out his followers one by one, always staying just out of their reach.

Four men were following the lad. They gathered to team up on him when Bartholomew suddenly disappeared. The men looked around, baffled, but Ransom noted a girl with loose hair walking by, her cloak hood pulled around her, her eyes to the ground.

Ransom smiled. Silently, he followed the girl. She dashed into a side alley, and a moment later Bartholomew appeared, shoulders erect, running with the girl's brown cloak in his hand. On reaching the edge of the city, he stopped and gave a low whistle.

A black horse came trotting up, and without assistance, Bartholomew swung into the saddle, galloping off into the open countryside.

Casually, Ransom made his way back into town to retrieve his horse. The four men were still standing in the square, looking through the crowd. Despite their disguises, they were not well hidden. They were the men of Lord Raburn.

Lord Raburn had a reputation. Anyone when asked, would tell you he was one of the kindest men alive, a good noble, and highly thought of. In the shadows of the taverns, in the heart of the dark, the truth barely dared to whisper. For three years, King Fredric had been fighting in the Crusades, and Lord Raburn had climbed from a barely noticed noble to Prince Alfred's lord protector. He was feared and that reverently, save for the few who dared to poke holes into the kingdom he was trying to create.

There were two particular aching points at this time. An anonymous person who sang only in the dark and always referred to himself as Song Lark, who spread all kinds of nasty rumors that harked closer to the truth than people claimed to believe…and a girl.

A single girl shouldn't have been much of a problem, if she had been a regular damsel, but Ransom knew she wasn't. He smiled as he remembered his commission.

"Find her, earn her trust, and bring her to me." That he would do.

At the edge of town, he mounted his horse and followed the trail. It would be a good half hour before

Raburn's men would figure out they had been fooled. They were too stubborn and sure of their own strength to believe that a mere girl could elude them. What other reason could there be? She had been on the loose for six months and was still unscathed, uncornered, and uncaught.

Casually following the trail, he entered the cool shadows of the woods. He hadn't realized how hot it was until the trees shaded him from the burning sun.

The forest seemed to be steeped in a mossy breeze, and there was a thin, chuckling brook running through it. Bartholomew knelt at the brook's side, taking a deep draft from his canteen. Laying it aside, he bent over the brook and splashed water over his face, rubbing the back of his neck.

I should just call Bartholomew a girl. It's obvious. That, or he is a hopeless dandy, Ransom thought as he watched her adjust the hat sideways, then straight, then to the other side. Now it seemed to sit in a satisfactory manner.

As she reached back for her canteen, she turned fully around, her hand seeming to rest casually on her dagger. Ransom knew better; it was a trained action.

"I didn't fancy that I would see you again," said the youth, quirking a half wry smile.

Time to make fiction fact. "I almost thought that you were a girl." Ransom let on with a chuckle as he dismounted, leading his horse towards the stream

"What?" the youth tried to keep the look of surprise off his face. "Are you daft?" he said, plunging his canteen beneath the surface so it would fill faster—trying not to act edgy.

"Of course I am. You are a very good player, but it won't see you through. You keep too clean; someone is bound to notice. Oh, and cut your hair so you don't have to keep it under your hat all of the time. It seems rude."

"Thank you for the advice. I just might take it," he said sarcastically, rising to his feet and securing the cover of the canteen.

"You fight well, but you use too many dance steps. Like that twirl you made. It reminded me of a girl whirling around in a pretty dress."

"What? Dance steps? You *are* out of your head, sir."

"Nonetheless, it proves to be a valuable asset to you. Next time you fight, don't show feelings in your eyes; it might give people the wrong impression."

"You are one sore loser."

"You are desperate. You need the money. What

else are you after?"

"None of your business," Bartholomew said, stalking towards his horse and securing his saddlebags

"It becomes my business when you take half my earnings."

"Then take the money; I want nothing to do with it!" Bartholomew tossed it arrogantly at Ransom's feet.

Ransom ignored the coins and stepped beside the youth. "I asked you a question and I expect an answer."

"Well, I don't expect to answer it," the youth said, beginning to mount.

Ransom grabbed Bartholomew by the belt, pulling him down onto his feet.

"Let me go!" he said, turning around to face his opponent.

The swordsman tightened his grip on the belt, pulling the youth into himself. He held him there as the youth squirmed against his firm hold.

"How dare you insult me in such a fashion!" said the lad, his face turning bright red.

"Those are awfully high words for such a lad. In fact, they sound very much like a lady's. Holding you this close would only be an insult to a lady, you know."

There was a flash of metal. A dagger pressed into Ransom's throat.

"Let me go." Bartholomew's eyes were cold and calculating. His mouth pulled tight.

The swordsman released the belt and backed away. Dagger in hand, Bartholomew stepped toward his horse.

"Don't forget your earnings," Ransom reminded.

"They aren't mine," he said with a quick mount. "Hya!" The youth disappeared into the forest.

Ransom looked after her with a smile, then glanced down at the small boot prints. Every sense told him it was a girl. What he had just held in his arms was a girlish figure, despite the baggy outline declaring otherwise. Yes, it was a girl. A girl in desperate need; one who was willing to challenge men to earn her keep and tell the truth. This was the one he was on the hunt for. How long would it take to earn her trust?

"Come on, boy, let's follow her." Mounting, he turned his horse to track her down.

CHAPTER 2

Her trail was easy to follow. It was apparent that she didn't consider him a threat, or maybe she was just trying to get distance between them.

Breaking out of the forest, he saw her cutting across the rolling hills of the open countryside. Pulling his horse to a halt, he paused. He had discovered her, but to win her trust was a different matter. She had eluded him twice. He had to be careful not to spook her, or he would never obtain his goal.

He pulled his horse to a standstill within the rim of the forest's shadow. As she reached the crest of a hill, she pulled up harshly. The horse reared pawing the air. Changing directions, she was flying back towards the forest, hugging the neck of her horse; a moment later, four men came riding over the ridge.

They didn't even bother tracking her! No wonder they can't find her. Maybe she'll need my help after all.

By the time she reached the forest, they were breathing down her neck. She plunged through the wood, her only purpose to flee, surmounting whatever obstacle came her way.

Ransom turned his horse and followed; this he had to see.

Weaving like a serpent in and out of the trees, she kept their crossbows at bay as the arrows flashed into trees, nearly grazing the horse and rider. Ransom's breath caught as he saw a felled tree across the way. It was far too high to jump and too low for a rider to get safely beneath, even if the horse could.

Ransom watched as she swung both legs to one side of the saddle. Lying sideways over her horse, her head hung above the ground. A stray branch swept off the hat, letting her hair tumble free; it just brushed the earth. Passing under the tree, she pulled herself upright and swung smoothly back into the saddle. A moment later, one of Raburn's men tried to pass underneath. Leaning close to the neck of his beast, he was swept off his horse and fell into an unconscious spiral. Only three pursued her now.

A black-fletched arrow from the bow of Raburn's men found a target in the horse's neck, sending the galloping steed to its knees. The girl tumbled from the saddle and rolled onto the ground. She didn't move.

Ransom pulled up his horse, wondering what he should do. The men passed her and then returned. Two dismounted while the third stayed on his horse.

"She's out cold," one of the men murmured, kicking her legs.

"Finally. Never thought we would catch her with such little fuss."

"Won't she be surprised when she wakes up?"

"Hurry up, you two. We have six months' time to make up for."

As one man bent down to tie her hands, there was an unexpected movement. A flash of leg landed in one man's stomach, while a flying arm caught the second man in the chin as she rolled to her feet and pulled out her sword to face the rider.

He laughed. "You really think you can take on a man?"

"We'll see if I can," she challenged, panting for breath.

The captain dismounted and pulled out his sword. The other two were still moaning on the ground.

He tapped her sword with his. She didn't flinch at the metallic sound but looked him dead in the eyes. The captain approached her slowly, his blade touching her raised sword. She let it come down to the hilt of her blade.

The captain laughed, "You are a foolish one." He lunged for her core.

Sweeping aside the blow, the girl jumped away.

"Try and kill me again and you will regret it," she threatened through clenched teeth, her eyes flashing, sword held out.

"Oh, to the contrary, my dear Annabeth; I'll enjoy it very much."

There was no foreplay of swords, no attempt to hide the purpose of his mission. It was an onslaught to her death.

She only wanted to survive.

A minute more, and the other men recovered drawing their swords and joining the fight. She met their blades without fear blow for blow.

Without warning, her sword went flying and she fell to her knees as a sword point came to her neck. Looking up to them, she did not beg for mercy or quarter.

"What should I do with you?" sneered the leader.

"As you please. Death is not too good for me," she answered calmly.

He twisted the blade against her throat, tracing her neckline. She winced as he prodded the sword into her neck. She closed her eyes.

There was a cry of dismay, and the sword at her neck quivered. Annabeth opened her eyes.

The man named Ransom, who she had fought in the square, stood there, his dagger at the leader's throat. He was pulling the dagger out of the captain's belt.

"Are you really going to kill a girl for such a simple offense? I know wearing boys' clothing is a punishable crime, but death seems a little severe," he said calmly.

"She, sir, is a wanted criminal."

Ransom laughed. "She! A wanted criminal? Yes. I see it. The hardened lines about her face, the refusal to yield at your command. See that look on her face? It is indeed the sign of an impossible child. But only a child, sir, and a girl at that. Let her go."

"There are a thousand pieces in good gold coin on her head."

"No head is worth that, except the silly bard, Song Lark. Why would someone want to kill a minstrel, anyways?"

"She, is in league with the Song Lark, who is a conniving traitor to the crown."

Slowly melting back from the blade that licked her neck, Annabeth moved towards her sword, which lay just out of reach. The men's swords were trained on the stranger, so surprised by his unexpected appearance they did not notice her subtle movements. In a flash, she had her sword. Without hesitation, she let it sing through the air, sending the captain's sword out of his hand. Raburn's two other men turned towards her as she rose to her feet.

"On your guard!" Ransom shouted pushing the leader in her direction while throwing two daggers at the same time into the other men.

As the leader barreled down towards her, she held up her sword in defense. It ran him through. Cringing from her sword, Annabeth dropped it and turned away, a wave of sickness washing over her.

There was a long moment of silence. Then she heard the subtle crunch of the underbrush beneath his boots. His stance was strong: hands on hips, head cocked to once side. She could feel all that with her eyes closed. She didn't really want to open them again, to see the men around her. Dead men. She had only seen one before, and it was something she would rather forget. Still, it was one of the reasons that kept her going when she wondered why. A shiver escaped up her spine. Suddenly she felt weak; the adrenaline was gone. Her stomach turned, reminding her there was nothing in it but water. It rose in her throat and she forced it back down, shoving the thought of the bodies out of her mind.

"What is your real name?" he asked.

"Annabeth," she answered with a slight choke in her voice.

"You are *that* Annabeth?" he asked incredulously.

"Yes," she answered, opening her eyes and turning to face him. "What are you going to do? Turn me in?" she asked, realizing she felt too weak to run even if she wanted to.

"Why would I do that? I just saved your life."

"There is a price on my head. You heard: a thousand pieces of gold."

"You don't seem like an outlaw to me. What did you do?"

"I ran away," Annabeth answered with a touch of sarcasm. She was fighting to find her strength; her inner armor had slipped away.

"That is your crime? Running away. From what are you running, may I ask?"

"The less you know, the better," she answered flatly.

"You aren't very grateful."

"Just because you rescued me doesn't mean I have to be grateful."

"It doesn't?"

"No," she said, turning to look at him fully. Then she glanced down. It was too much to take. Her body revolted, sending up the fresh liquid she had taken in. Going to a nearby tree, she leaned against it for support, trying to hold it in. The attempt was useless. A minute later she sank to her knees, resting her head against the tree.

Closing her eyes, Annabeth breathed deeply, but it felt as if the very air was suffocating her, as if she could never breathe enough again. At that moment, she couldn't have cared less what happened next. She wanted it over with. All she wanted was to be free from being hunted and haunted. Her body was in need of rest, and she was never going to get it at this rate.

Her stomach rumbled restlessly.

Unexpectedly, Annabeth found an arm around her tender stomach. She winced as he pulled her to her feet. Her hands found his arm and tried to push it away.

"Hey," his voice was soft and slightly reproving.

Annabeth knew she was too weak to fight and let her body sag against him. Ransom placed the canteen to her lips.

"Take only a sip," he warned.

The cold water trickled down her throat and hit

her stomach with a twisting pang that threatened to send it back up.

"When was the last time you ate?" he asked, his voice hovering softly next to her ear. There was a touch of tenderness in it that pulled at her heart.

Annabeth shook her head. She was too weak to get her head clear. Her heart shouldn't feel anything. She needed to silence whatever that flutter was.

"Do you refuse to tell me?" he whispered, a sternness entering his voice. *That* Annabeth knew how to handle.

"Two days ago."

"I have some bannock in my bag. You can have that."

"I can't eat anything right now. I would only lose it."

Annabeth pushed away his arm from around her waist and walked shakily to the tree, leaning her back against it. Slipping her hands behind her, she dug her fingernails into the papery bark.

"Well, you should change, at least, and get out of those miserable clothes," he said with a nod towards her shirt.

Glancing down, her stomach wrenched again. Blood stained it. A chill ran through her spine, and goosebumps ran down her arms. "I have clothes in my saddlebag," she thought out loud.

"I'll get them for you," he said, turning away.

"I can do it," she said, moving from the tree.

But he was already there, kneeling down and freeing her saddlebags from beneath the body of her horse.

Annabeth looked at her horse. She was already gone. Tears rose in her eyes. The hours they had spent together—the memories floated through her mind's eye. She blinked them away.

Where was the armor that was supposed to protect her heart?

She placed her head against the tree and looked up into the sky. It was blue, the color of her father's eyes. Suddenly, the armor slipped into place. She, Annabeth, would survive. For him, she would go on, and someday maybe he too would be free. Maybe someday she wouldn't have to run from the "law." The energy of pure will surged forward through her veins.

I will be strong. I will go on.

Ransom reached into her saddlebag. What he pulled out surprised even him.

"A dress?"

"You know I am a girl, so what's surprising about that?" The tenderness that had been in her voice as she rested against him was gone. She was the boy he had met in the square, bold and daring.

"I just thought you would have gotten rid of all the evidence. Wear this for now," he said, coming to her side, trying to look into her eyes that were fastened to the forest floor. "We'll tie our fortunes together. You need a protector, and I am available."

"I couldn't accept." She half laughed, half sighed, taking the dress and slipping sideways away from him.

"Why on earth not?" he said, sidestepping and putting his arm against the tree, blocking her escape.

Her eyes raised to his, clashing with a glittering revolt in them. For a moment, she challenged his; then she dropped them again. "It is just that I…you don't know what you are dealing with. I have been on the run for over six months. He won't give up until I am caught or dead."

"And who is he that won't give up?"

"If you don't know, he can't harm you."

"They could have."

"'Cause you stuck around. If you hadn't been around..."

"You would have been captured by them."

"I would have been long gone if you hadn't delayed me with all your chatter by the river," she said, slipping beneath his arm.

He caught her and spun her to face him, holding Annabeth's arm firmly but not sternly.

"Annabeth, I don't think you realize it, but a girl should be held in a man's arms and loved and cherished, not on her knees with a sword to her neck. What are you doing out here with a sword by your side and a bounty on your head?"

Annabeth blushed hotly at his words. "Turn me in, and you will find out," she challenged him.

"I don't think so."

"Then go away. This isn't your battle to fight. It is mine." She turned from him and walked away.

"How do you expect to win a fight if you aren't willing to kill?"

"I was ready to kill you earlier."

"Ready to kill is not willing to kill. You might have harmed me for attempting to unmask you, but you will never kill those who already know your disguise."

"When you kill his men, you make him angry."

"Who is he?"

She turned and walked further away. Ransom followed.

"I asked you a question."

Annabeth whirled around. "And I suppose you will expect an answer."

"How do you expect to win a fight if you aren't willing to kill?" he asked again.

She cocked her head to one side.

"I'll disarm them," she said with a shrug of her shoulder.

"So you will disarm three men that come after you, and none of them will retrieve their weapon while the others close in? How long can you fight? There were three of them. How long do you think you could have lasted against them?"

Annabeth refused to look at him.

"Really, how long?"

"I don't know. You didn't give me a chance."

"Give you a chance—what kind of chance were you looking for? Death? That is always a great opportunity; it comes only once in a lifetime, you know. You can't outrun them and you can't outfight them. What do you really expect to do?"

"I don't know, I—*There were four!*" The sudden high note in her voice, her eyes wide in fear, told him there was a problem.

Ransom didn't hesitate; pulling out his sword, he whirled around, his blade ready to catch whatever came his way.

The sword of the fourth man was upraised, descending down on him, ready to separate Ransom in half. A moment later, the man lay dead and Ransom's sword was crimson with the tide of someone else's life.

He turned back to Annabeth.

"I am going to get changed," she whispered, stepping away from him.

Ransom nodded in approval. He would get the horses ready.

CHAPTER 3

When Annabeth returned, she was carrying her clothes gingerly. The bloodstain was well hidden. Ransom had taken all the horses to the riverbank to be watered.

"I thought that horse would be close to the one you had," he said, with a nod to the white horse that stood at the end of the line.

Annabeth tried to hide her smile. That was the one she would have chosen for herself.

Going to her saddlebags, she prepared to hide the bloodstained clothes from her sight.

"You aren't going to put your clothes in there like that, are you?"

"What's wrong with that?"

"You'll never get the blood out."

"I don't plan to wear them again."

"Just the same," he said, coming to her side. Taking the clothes from her hands, he went to the river and submerged them, then nodded to his horse. "There is bannock in the saddlebag. I suggest you eat some before we get under way."

Annabeth reached into his saddlebag and found a white cloth wrapped around the bannock. Pulling out a piece, she nibbled carefully at it. She didn't trust her stomach much yet.

Leaning against the tree, she watched him curiously.

"What are you staring at?" Ransom asked.

"I have never seen a man wash clothes before."

"Really? We do it all the time when there are no women around. Or at least when we need to."

"That must explain it," she said, sinking to the ground, closing her eyes, and resting her head against the tree. She was worn clean through, but she had to keep her eyes open...

"Tired?"

Annabeth forced her eyes open. "Not really."

"You can say so if are, you know."

"I know."

Ransom turned back to the clothes, fiddling with nothing for a time. When he turned back to see how she was doing, her eyes were closed again, shoulders relaxed. He returned to his washing and began to wring out the clothes.

In a moment, Annabeth got to her feet. "We need to go."

"What?"

"We need to go." Her voice was explicitly urgent. "Don't you feel it?"

"Feel what?"

"You'll know. Now, if you value your life, I suggest you come. He'll want you dead the moment he finds out you killed his men," she said, swinging with ease into her saddle.

Annabeth took the wet clothes from his hands and tucked them into her empty saddlebags. "Are you coming? Because I am not waiting."

"I don't get what all the fuss is about."

"Stay here and you'll find out," she said, glancing around. She pushed her horse forward into the river and started up the stream.

Something about her words unsettled him. He glanced around the forest; everything seemed normal. Just the same, he wasn't about to let her slip through his grasp. If she felt like moving on, he would follow. Mounting, he followed her into the river, pulling one of the guard's horses after him—it could come in handy.

For a long time, they rode up the river, emerging

several times. They traipsed through the forest only to come back to the river. Weaving on and off the roads and trails, Annabeth kept leading them to the river.

"Is it your purpose to drive whoever you are running from absolutely mad?"

"He already is," she whispered, and continued on. Coming to a branch in the river, she took it. Suddenly, the river disappeared into the ground.

"Where are we going now?"

"We follow the river."

"Are you crazy?"

Turning to him, she smiled "There are steps. Just be careful; it is easy to slip. It's best if you lead the horses," she said, slipping to the ground.

Her horse balked as she led it forward. "I know you don't know me, but I need you to trust me," she whispered. "Come on." The horse followed with great hesitance.

In a few minutes, they were walking in complete darkness, following the sound of horses' hooves on the floor. He was glad that she had a white horse, since even in the darkness he could somewhat see it. Or was that some ghostly shadow that was leading him to his death? Water soaked into his boots, much to his great discomfort.

In a few minutes, she halted. There was the sound of steel and flint striking together, and a light slowly flickered to life. Annabeth lit a small torch, and his eyes almost hurt adjusting to the light.

He watched as Annabeth shook her head, as if a shiver ran through her shoulders and down her spine. She didn't like the darkness.

She led the way. Ransom suppressed the question. *"Do you know where you are going?"* It was obvious she did, even if he felt rather lost. He was dealing with something he had never known before. No wonder the girl had a reputation for slipping into thin air. He would have never guessed that she could disappear into a hole in the ground.

They walked for a considerable distance, a new torch appearing just before the old one died out. *How long has she been here? How does she know this area so well?*

In a little while, the last torch died and they walked forward. The light grew until they came around the bend. There was light: full, rich, blinding, and hot after the cool dampness of the cave.

Annabeth swung easily up into the saddle and rode out of the cave. The water had all but disappeared, and they rode out into a thick forest. She pulled to a halt and waited for him to come alongside.

She looked up at him. "Where are we going to go now?"

Ransom raised an eyebrow. "What do you mean, 'where are we going to go now'? Don't you know where you are going?"

"I am not going that way," she said with a nod towards the southeast.

Her demeanor was relaxed; there was nothing tense about her. She seemed almost as if she could laugh.

"I have one question. Where did the river go?"

"There is a place where the river splits away. You don't want to end up there, unless you want to swim for a lifetime—or what is left of it."

"Did you discover that by yourself?"

Annabeth didn't answer as she looked vaguely about, then turned to him. "Where are we going?"

Ransom smiled. "All right, if you insist." He led her directly north.

The ride was silent. Annabeth was too busy watching the countryside for Lord Raburn's men to speak, and Ransom was content to let it be that way, although he did have to look back once in a while just to know she was there.

As night began to fall, he looked for a place to camp. Ransom found the perfect place in a small wooded hollow behind a gently sloping hill. When he stopped, Ransom was surprised that he didn't need to speak a word before Annabeth dismounted and began taking care of her horse. Smiling, he dismounted and did the same.

"Do you want to light a fire?" he asked her.

"It's too warm, and there is no need to let people know we are here. I don't think the wild animals will bother us."

Ransom nodded. It seemed reasonable enough. Gathering leaves, she made herself a bed beneath a pine's low spreading branches. Laying down the horse blanket, she took out her cloak and made as if ready to go to sleep.

"Aren't you hungry?"

"A little, I guess."

"I still have bannock."

"But there is no knowing how long we'll be hiding. We may need all that we can spare."

"Have you forgotten I have coin? I can buy anything we need."

"If there is someone willing to sell."

"Have you ever met anyone who isn't willing?"

“If they are afraid that Lord Raburn...” She dropped her sentence and looked off into the distance as if she heard something.

“You were saying something about Lord Raburn?” Ransom said pointedly.

“Hmm? Oh, I forgot what I was going to say. You said something about food?”

"Yes, I did."

“It sounds good,” she said with a smile.

Ransom looked at her skeptically, and handed her a piece of bannock. Going to her tree, she sat down and leaned comfortably against it. He sat on a fallen log. “It would feel much more like I was actually in company with someone if you sat out here.”

“Why would I want to do that?”

Ransom gave her a look that said, *Why not?*

“I like trees,” she answered with a shrug.

“So, who is this Lord Raburn? I have heard him spoken of, but I really don’t know who he is.”

“What have you heard about him?”

“He is Prince Alfred’s lord protector, a goodly noble, left in charge of the kingdom while the king is off fighting in the crusades.”

“You are a foreigner, aren’t you?” she said, her eyes narrowing slightly.

"What would make you say that?"

"You speak the same language, but you know nothing of what is going on."

"I travel a lot."

"Well, that is no excuse. How did he become Lord Protector? Do you know?"

"They say that Lord Gambury died of a heart trauma in his sleep or something like that."

Annabeth's eyes slitted as she examined him. "That is the common belief."

"Do you know better?"

Annabeth opened her eyes wider. "I said it was common. I did not say I knew better—but there are rumors," she said, lowering her eyes but still meeting his. "Rumors that are only sung by Song Lark."

"And does anyone know who this Song Lark is?"

"For that, there are rumors too. Some say he is a ghost, but I prefer to think he is real. A minstrel fool, without a brain, but really a master of disguise with a mind. That is why I like to think no one has found out who he is."

"Ah, and that is why there is a price on his head."

"Wouldn't you want someone dead who is spreading false rumors about you? And such hideous ones too, like…

Oh, fear the wrath of Raburn,
Or he thy blood will churn.
He hath no heart but a stone,
And when he singeth, he hath no tone.

Isn't that ridiculous?" she almost laughed.

"Quite. I would want someone dead if they sang that about me, too."

"Now, sir who asks me so many questions, may I ask you a few?"

"I doubt that I will have many answers, but I'll see what I can manage."

"How do you know I am not willing to kill?"

"Your eyes."

Her brow wrinkled, her eyes asking for an explanation.

"Life is precious to you; you'd rather your own life was taken than someone else lose theirs—but you will fight to the death to live." Ransom paused. "Would you really let him kill you today?"

"The ransom on my head is for me alive, not dead. He was threatening idly. He is—was—a coward. If it ever changes to dead or alive, then I will have to worry. But why have you chosen to live by the sword? You are obviously skilled. Why don't you go into the army or some sort of notion?"

"All they want is a war for the Holy Land. I'll give up my life for no religious promenade. Some people claim it is a worthy cause, but…" Ransom shook his head.

"So, you have no faith?"

"What is there to have faith in?"

Annabeth didn't answer the question with her words, but her eyes spoke and a tenderness rose in them. It was a tenderness that knew something—something she guarded carefully.

Ransom answered his own question for her; he didn't like the look in her eyes. "The only person I have faith in is myself. Who else will look out for me? In the army, in a battle, the only person you can depend on is yourself."

"So, why do you want to help me? You don't believe Raburn is bad, and yet you help me when you have no idea as to why."

"Maybe you could give me a reason—other than the fact that you are a girl in distress."

Annabeth's eyes narrowed again. "So you abide by the laws of chivalry, even if you aren't a knight?"

"They are good general rules for any man to live by. But give me a reason to make it my creed."

"As to reasons, I have none to give other than that

I am fighting my own little war, for reasons no one can know."

"And if they know?"

"They die. In the morning I suggest we take our separate ways. We aren't too far from the border. I suggest you cross back over it and be safe."

"And if I don't?"

"I am no knight, sir. I can offer you no protection."

"But I can offer you some."

"That is an offer I still must refuse, I am afraid."

"Well, I'll give you the night to think on it."

She smiled slightly. "Fair enough."

"Good night."

"Night," she answered, pulling her cloak over her shoulders and lying down.

Ransom sighed. It had been a long day, but things were looking promising.

CHAPTER 4

Annabeth lay perfectly still, breathing deeply. She kept one eye open, listening as Ransom readied for sleep a short distance away. Taking off his sword, he lay down, pulling his cloak about him. At the sound of his deep breathing, she relaxed and fell into a light sleep. She would wait for morning.

When the stars glittered their brightest in the darkness before the dawn, Annabeth slipped to her feet. Noiselessly, she approached Ransom. Standing over him, she pulled his dagger smoothly from the sheath. Taking the damp strips of cloth she had sliced from the bottom of the shirt Ransom had washed, Annabeth tied his ankles together first, then slipped two separate strips around his hands and slowly started drawing them together behind his back.

Ransom awoke.

He bolted to fight, but her knee dug deeply into his back just below his neck, and she pulled his hands tightly together, wrapping and tying knots as she went, despite his struggles to free himself.

"Damp fabric is always hard to untie when done

in knots. It's hard enough to tie as it is."

"What are you going to do with me?"

"Men who live by the sword—die by the sword. I suggest when you get out of your bonds that you head for the border, unless you have some sort of death wish. If you don't mind, I am going to take back my earnings. Since you have a second horse, you can sell that and it will more than make up for what you lost to me," she said, freeing him of some of the coins at his waist and rising to her feet.

Ransom rolled over to face her. "You are making a mistake."

"I am saving your life," she said, sinking his dagger deep into the tree above her head and well out of his reach. Then, taking his sword belt, she climbed up into the tree and hung it also out of reach before dropping to the ground.

Ransom glared at her and a smile pulled at the corner of her mouth.

"Godspeed to you, sir. May He keep you and your noble sword safe. Thank you for everything you did, but I cannot accept your help. This is my war and I must live or die by the results."

Going to his saddlebag, she took bannock and her small pouch of earnings and nodded towards the hill.

"A little ways that way there is a farmhouse. I am sure that she would be willing to sell you whatever you want to eat."

Ransom's brow wrinkled. "How did you…?"

"Godspeed, sir. Farewell."

Annabeth swung easily into the saddle, and, tapping the horse's side, they broke into a trot and disappeared into the darkness.

Ransom was furious. How had he found, followed, and been so close to her, only to lose her again? Was it possible?

He wrenched his bonds. Yes, it was possible.

I, Ransom, the best bounty hunter…

That thought he let slip: apparently not the best at everything. His commission slipped painfully through his mind.

"Find her, earn her trust, and bring her to me, for her father's sake."

"Well, sir. I promised two months, but since it has taken me almost a month just to find her…" He sighed, testing the bonds again. His hands were fastened tightly, and pulling on the wet knots only made them tighter. Drawing his knees into his chest, he pushed his arms down behind his back, around his legs, and over his bound ankles.

He then looked at the knot.

It was like nothing he had ever seen before. It was a series of wrapping and weavings mingled with knots of several varieties. He looked for the ends in the light of the grey dawn. They were somewhere, all right, but where in the mess, he wasn't quite sure. He glanced up at his dagger, sunk so deeply into the bark of the tree. There wasn't even a hint of the blade.

If I could only get to that, I would be out of this in a twinkling.

He moved to stand, but his tied ankles made him stumble. Leaning forward, he went to untie the knot. It was firmly fastened behind his ankles, with no easy way to access it. Flushed with anger and resentment, Ransom pushed himself against the tree and inched to a standing position. Turning, he faced the tree and pulled his dagger out with a jerk that almost sent him into a backwards tumble. Placing the now-dulled dagger in his mouth, he sawed through the damp cloth. At last he was free–at least partly.

"Annabeth, when I find you…!" he threatened under his breath as he cut through his ankle bonds. "I'll—I'll…" He paused. He wasn't sure *what* he would do. He had to keep her safe. *"Bring her to me for her father's sake."*

"Sir, did you have any clue?" Ransom kicked his legs free. He had ground to make up.

Climbing the tree, he took down his sword and fastened it to his side. He dropped to the ground, carried his saddle from the far side of camp to his horse tethered on the very opposite end, saddling his horse, he mounted.

His stomach rumbled. He could travel on an empty stomach, but a filled one was better. He would have to find that farmhouse. As he rode in the direction that she had signified, he found his horse's gait strange. Dismounting, he found to his utter and complete disgust that a shoe was loose.

"Did you do that all by yourself or did she help you?" he asked his horse, hands on hips. The horse didn't seem to deem it necessary to reply as he looked blankly at Ransom. He switched mounts, leading his misshod companion. Time was slipping away with precious swiftness.

In a minute he spotted the farmhouse and pulled his horse to a halt in front of the door. As he was dismounting, the door opened and a round woman appeared. She chuckled under her breath as he stepped forward to introduce himself.

"Are you Ransom?"

He stopped in his tracks, startled.

She laughed at the look on his face. "She said you would be by and that I should have this ready to give you." The woman waved a sack at him.

Suspicious, Ransom stepped forward and took it from her hands. He felt the hot bannock through the sack, and his mouth watered. "My husband is a decent farrier, by the way, and he's in the shed out back, and she said I was to give this to you, too," she said, handing him a second but smaller sack. Ransom opened it to find it filled with dried meat and smoked cheese.

"How much do I owe you?"

"The girl paid for it. Now go in the back; he is waiting."

The sound of a hammer striking metal steered Ransom in the right direction. Water sizzled and steamed up as the man placed a glowing metal object in a bucket of water. Looking up, the man saw him coming.

"I was just getting ready to come after you. She said if you didn't appear by the time I was ready for you to come a lookin'."

"Well, I am here now," Ransom said between

clenched teeth. *How on earth could she do this to me? Why did she have to be so know-it-all irritating? And why, of all people, am I sent after her?*

In a minute the man was working on the horse's shoe, setting it properly into place. Ransom waited impatiently, reminding himself that he was actually saving time by having a good horse instead of dragging one with a loose shoe around.

"There you go, sir; that will be three coppers."

Ransom fished the money out of his money pouch and handed it to the man.

"Do you know which way she went?"

"Aye."

Ransom waited. The man went back to work.

"Are you going to answer my question?"

"Nay."

"I will give you three silver pieces if you tell me where she went."

The man looked up at him, doubtful.

Frustrated to the core, Ransom pulled out the money and laid it on the table. "I am her friend; I need to know where she went. She is in grave danger and I need to know."

The man glanced at it and nodded.

"Where did she go?"

"That-a-way," he said with a nod to the west.

"Are you sure?"

He nodded and mutely took the money off the table, putting it in his pocket.

Ransom walked in that direction and picked up her trail. It was hers all right, and pretty fresh. With hope riding high in his heart, he followed her. *It should be easy to catch up.* However, by noon he had lost her trail and the only person he passed was a decrepit and bent elderly lady with a horse suffering from a bad case of mange pulling a cart. He searched the road the surrounding areas, but to no avail. She was gone. She and her trail had vanished into thin air.

CHAPTER 5

For the next two weeks Ransom followed any phantom news of Annabeth, traipsing all over the country hither and thither, yon and aft, with little success in finding her precise whereabouts and disguise. He was one week into the second month of the time he had promised to have her, and now he was completely baffled with his mission. His plans weren't working at all. The thwarting only made him cling to her trail hotly; searching, watching, waiting for her appearance.

Raburn's men were doubled. With her traveling with a supposed accomplice, she was now an even higher threat, and they were searching for her thoroughly.

Notorious descriptions were hung everywhere, claiming she was a dangerous criminal and should be brought to justice. Even with the large reward on her head, little effort was made on the people's part to have anything to do with her. They didn't dare help her, but they weren't about to turn her in, either. Let Raburn chase her around and leave the rest of them in peace.

Daily prayers for their king's return were offered. He was still off in the Holy Land fighting the crusades, while Prince Alfred's lord protector wreaked havoc on the land. Had he heard their pleas? Had the letters that begged for his return reached him; or was only Lord Raburn's news getting through to him, along with the Prince's missives which were overseen by the lord protector himself?

It was true that Prince Alfred was a public captive. Smiling, joyful, but certainly kept in hand and guarded with the greatest care by Lord Raburn.

The notorious Song Lark struck up a few new tunes claiming rash ideas in the midnight's darkest hours, strumming on his bold lute with courage, telling of fame and faults of those at court and countryside.

One of his latest horrifying truths ran something like this:

My name is Song Lark.
Oh, I pray thee, hark.
Listen to my words with care.
There is a fox within our lair.
He is handsome, he is bold,
He is dressed in yellow gold.
But he hath set for thee a snare;
Oh, our beloved prince, beware.

He hath cut the necks of nobles,
Yours he shall cut with no foibles.
He wants to make you cold as stone,
To take your throne to be his own.
Oh, prince, my prince, beware,
There is a fox within your lair.

The rage that poured out over this tune was large as Raburn's men turned out in full force. Ransom's search became much more stealthy, hidden, and urgent. He needed to find Annabeth.

His discovery of her was unexpected. He was riding along the road when she darted out in front of him across the path and into the forest beyond, with six men hot on her horse's heels.

Her white horse was foaming with sweat; theirs were fresh and strong. He immediately joined in the chase, taking up the rear without being noticed. In a clear spot in the forest, one man came riding up beside her, laying his hands on her waist in attempt to pull her off her horse. In a moment, her dagger flashed—cutting his arm. He fell from his horse with an agonized cry. Placing the dagger back in her belt, she whirled around with sword in hand, cutting down the next man that dared to come near her.

Ransom withdrew his sword and started working

his way toward the front, taking men down one at a time as he neared her.

Two men approached her at once, and she tumbled off the back of her horse to avoid their fatal blows. She drew one man into combat, using her horse as a shield for her back, as the other approached her. In order to get at Annabeth, he had to dismount. She held them off well as the third man parlayed Ransom into a corner, which he fatally thrust himself out of. Turning to help Annabeth, he watched as she rushed between them, hesitating for a moment, then leapt aside as both blades thrust forward with deadly intent: the killing blow that was meant for her taking their lives.

Annabeth stood sideways and turned to look at him. “So you've come to finish me off, have you?” she asked, her eyes glittering with an unusual brightness, while her face seemed ashen pale in comparison.

He didn't answer, but stepped forward.

“I thought you would have gone home.”

“I never take advice I don't ask for.”

“Are you that desperate to be a wanted man? For you are one, though no one has a clue to who you might be. I suggest you go while you still have a chance.”

“I am here to offer you my protection.”

"I am not used to taking protection I don't ask for."

Ransom smiled as she threw his own words back at him. "So that makes us more alike; we are both wanted, both excellent swords people, and both have nothing better to do."

"I have much better things to be doing. They just don't allow me time for it." She nodded with a shiver towards the dead men. "Now, if you will excuse me, I should be going. You can have whatever loot you want from them."

She whistled softly and her horse came closer.

Ransom stepped to her side and whirled her around. "What exact–"

She let out an agonized cry of pain and dropped to the ground.

Then he saw it. Annabeth's left side was dripping with blood. *Her* blood. That was why she had only turned part of the way around to look at him.

"Annabeth," he said, dropping to her side.

"It's only a flesh wound," she whimpered, holding her left hand tightly over it.

"Let me see it."

"No," she ground out between her teeth.

"You can't go on like this."

Annabeth only closed her eyes; she was feeling lightheaded. Rising, he went to his saddlebags and pulled out one of the sacks he had been given to keep his food in. Digging into hers, he found the shirt with strips cut from the bottom: strips that had been stretched and then used to tie his hands and feet together.

"Lie down, Annabeth."

Too weak to resist the order she did his bidding, sending her head into a wild spin.

Taking the shirt, the softest and cleanest of all the materials, he pressured the wound with his left hand. Placing his knee on the large sack to hold it still, he cut long wide strips. Tying them together, he gently but firmly wrapped them around her waist.

Ransom laid his canteen gently on her lips. "Here, just a little bit."

She closed her eyes and laid her head on the ground, completely exhausted and weary.

"Are there any more men following you?" he asked in a whisper.

"I had just gotten well away from one band when I was found by them. I suggest you leave me to my fate. They will find me soon enough." Her voice seemed resigned to abandonment. She was preparing herself for death.

"I don't think so. Rest for a few minutes." He took her left hand and washed it free of blood.

Opening her eyes, she looked at him. "Thank you."

"Lie still."

Standing, Ransom looked and listened to the forest around them. There was something in the forest—something far, far away, but the threat was still real. She was so pale, but there was need for haste. He looked at her horse. It was worn out. Looking around, he chose a new horse that seemed steady and reliable and placed her saddle on it. They would need to ride separately if they were to move with any form of swiftness.

He waited as long as his gut would let him, then stirred her.

"Annabeth, I need you to stand. Here; take my hands and hold on tight." Ransom pulled Annabeth to her feet. She leaned against him, fighting the sense of nausea that swept around her and infiltrated every sense in her body. Her fingers gripped his doublet.

"Do you think you can ride?"

"Might as well give it a try," she whispered.

Ransom could not help his smile. She was

determined to escape them, no matter the cost. With a swift movement, he lifted her into the saddle. She buried her face in the horse's mane and was unable to move for several moments, but as he mounted into his saddle, she pushed herself to a seated position and took the reins.

Ransom looked at her. She was sitting up all right, but her eyes were blurred with pain and her face was pale and weary from loss of blood and a thousand other things. He would have to lead and watch her carefully.

CHAPTER 6

For over an hour they rode. Annabeth's eyes began to droop shut, heavy with weariness; she fought to keep them open, but they closed firmly for the last time. Ransom smiled sympathetically. Riding his horse as close to hers as possible, he pulled her foot from the stirrup. She didn't move. He swung his right leg over his saddle and placed it in her stirrup. In a moment he was sitting behind her, taking the reins from her moist hands and putting one arm around her, gently leaning her back against him.

Her head turned sideways against his shoulder. They rode together until the stars came out. Ransom pulled the horses to a stop. Gathering her into his arms, he slipped down from the horse's back. The landing jarred her, and Annabeth stirred with a whimper under her breath.

"Hush," he whispered in her ear, and she relaxed against him. Ransom smiled. Maybe he could earn her trust at last.

It was the middle of the night when a distressed voice woke him.

"No, don't. I don't want to. Let me go!"

He sat up and looked at her as the moon peeked through the clouds. Annabeth's face was bathed in sweat as she tossed her head one way, then another.

Taking his canteen, he went to her.

"Annabeth, shh. You are safe."

She flung her hand loosely at him, as if to drive him away, then it rested on her dagger, her weak hand trying to close around it.

Ransom's heart ached for her with a sudden pang. Even in her sleep she was ready to try to defend herself against him. When he placed his hand on Annabeth's to prevent the attack, he was bitterly surprised to find it hot with fever. He touched her forehead. She wasn't sweating from nightmares; Annabeth had a raging fever.

Ransom was furious with himself. *I should have watched her more carefully.* Going to his saddlebags, he pulled out a cloth and poured water over it. He returned to Annabeth and placed it on her forehead, then took her sword belt and dagger from her side. He wasn't about to take any risks.

For over an hour he tried to cool her temperature, but it only increased, and with the heat, the delirium and outbursts became more frequent. As he was fighting her fever, he tried to piece together what she was saying. She called for her father and for someone named Alf. Her feverish hands tried to keep him away, but they were so weak that they only spoke of her need of him.

He emptied both of their canteens, trying to bring down her fever, but to no avail. She was ill and he was out of immediate resources to help her. Somewhere nearby, a river went laughing over stones, seeming to mock him and his worries. Taking the canteens, he followed the sound.

It didn't take him long to find it. As he filled the canteens, he noticed that the river was wide and deep and the water bitingly cold as it drank from a mountain stream. He looked at the small canteens in his hands; he looked at the stream. He could only take so much to her, and it might eventually cool her off, but why not bring her to the river?

Ransom ran back to camp, took off his boots, and lifted the feverish Annabeth into his arms.

Walking back to the stream, he waded in carefully, holding his breath as it bit him in the dark. The rocks were slippery in the shallows where the water moved slowly. Deeper in was a firm, sandy bottom. He lowered her into the water.

Her fingernails raked across his shirt as her body rebelled with a fearful cry. Even in her delirium, she was trying to escape something. Ransom gritted his teeth as her fingers dug into him.

"No, no, I can't swim; help me!" It was a cry of fear as she writhed in his arms.

He held her tightly and whispered in her ear. "I have you, Annabeth. I have you; it's all right."

Her breath came in panicked gasps that caused her to hiccup.

Slower this time, he let her down into the water, only to have her panicked hands scrape him again.

"Annabeth!" he muttered between tightly clenched teeth.

A thought struck him, and he let her feet slip into the water, holding her tightly until her feet touched bottom. Slowly she relaxed, and her panicked breathing evened. He carefully pulled her out into deeper water, gauging how deep she could go and still touch the bottom. Finally, she was shoulder deep.

Unexpectedly, she spoke: "Alf."

She seemed to be waiting for a response.

"Yes?"

"You won't let me go, will you, Alf?"

Who is Alf? But Ransom leaned close to her ear

and whispered. "Of course not. I have you, Annabeth."

She relaxed, her head resting against his arm.

Ransom waited until his body began to spasm with cold. Gathering her into his arms, he walked back to the camp and built up the fire to warm and dry himself.

Her talking became even more frantic and disjointed. Ransom watched her with concern, as he learned much from her delirium and tried to piece it all together.

I'll not serve you. Don't leave me, mother; don't leave me. I won't fail you, father. I must go on. Let me be. No, no. I won't help you; let me go. God protect him. Song Lark, sing me something.

Suddenly, she screamed. Her feverish hands fought off the cloak, searching for something.

He killed him! Oh, God, he killed him! Help me; hide me. Oh, Lord, help me.

Annabeth was in a state of panic. Ransom caught her wild hands in his and gently pressed them to her side.

"You are safe, Annabeth," he repeated over and over again. However, from that moment on, the fever began to worsen. Just as he was getting ready to take her back to the river, she was covered in goosebumps and she was shivering as if in convulsions. The fight changed: he had to keep her warm. He drew her near the fire and covered her in her cloak, then his.

With a shiver and a sigh, she lay completely still.

For several moments Ransom wondered if he dare touch her.

Is she alive or dead? he wondered, leaning forward to touch her hand. She was not dead. Life still worked within her body, struggling though it was. She was weak and tired. Ransom looked at the sky with a sigh of relief. The soft colors of dawn were blushing on the horizon. Turning, he looked back to where they had come from. They would still be after her; Lord Raburn wanted her. It was his duty to earn her trust, come what may.

Saddling the horses, he gathered her in his arms. Placing her on the saddle and mounting behind her, he plunged the horses into the river downstream. They had to hurry; the border was not far. Once they crossed, she would be safe—perhaps against her will, but she would be safe. He would have kept his promise and it would all be over for him.

Near noon, she stirred. He held her close, hoping she wouldn't panic in fear.

Annabeth's eyes fluttered open. It was obvious by

the pain in her eyes that she was too tired and too ill to conceal that she felt unwell.

"Where am I?" she murmured between parched lips.

He stroked a hand over her hair, leaning her head against his shoulder. "You are safe with me."

A smile darted briefly through her eyes and slowly they closed again, weariness taking her against her will. He could feel her fighting it, her body almost rigid in its sleep, fighting for awareness, fighting to be ready.

Ransom shook his head and urged the horse into a canter. Every hour he changed horses. It was a hassle, but it saved the horses from being completely worn out. Only when darkness had settled over the land did Ransom stop and build a fire for the night.

Weary, Annabeth opened her eyes and sighed.

"Sleep well?"

"Well enough." She tried to sit up, but only landed on her back with a moan.

"Don't move. You are weak enough as it is. You need to save your strength."

For a long time, there was silence as he cooked over the open fire.

"Is it natural for the stars to spin wildly?" she asked, her voice tired.

"No."

"They won't stop."

"You need something to eat." He ladled the stew from the pot into a bowl and came to her side, offering her a spoonful.

"I can feed myself."

"Really? Well, you may give it a try," he said, placing the spoon in her hand.

Annabeth's hand shook as she tried to bring it to her mouth, and some of the broth dribbled down her cheek. She laughed at her lame effort, only to give a small cry as sharp pain shot through her body.

"It's only a flesh wound," she sighed.

"Flesh wounds can be deadly if not treated properly. You lost plenty of blood."

"Still," she said, trying to fight her way onto her elbow. Annabeth laid back in defeat.

Ransom was silent as he helped her eat, then he looked at her wound. The bleeding had stopped the night before, but the long ride had caused it to start again. He looked at her, dissatisfied.

"What is the matter?"

"You need rest, and you need it now."

"Where are we?"

"About three days from the border."

"Are we near the mountains?"

Ransom nodded.

"There is an abandoned shepherd's cottage up in the mountains. It's not too hard to find, but they have never looked for me there."

"Why?"

She smiled. "There is a mountain stream that comes out in a cave. It's pretty dark, but you go upstream until you reach the opening of the cave. It is barely walking room high."

"Another one of your disappearing tricks."

Annabeth smiled and closed her eyes. "Where is my sword?"

"It's safe," he answered.

"You aren't going to give it to me?"

"No. You have the luxury of being a damsel in distress."

Annabeth let out a sighing laugh, with a sniff of disgust.

"Get some sleep."

"Yes, sir."

CHAPTER 7

It was before dawn when Ransom woke and prepared them to leave camp. The border would have to wait; she was in no shape to ride for another three days unless he wanted to deliver her dead on his master's doorstep.

Annabeth leaned trustingly against him as she gave him directions to the mountain stream. At the mouth of the cave, they dismounted. It would be a low walk. He looked at Annabeth. Her eyes were steel-like in their desire. There was no way she could make it through the cave, wounded as she was. Standing up was killing her; leaning over would be her death.

"You ready?" she asked, a fortress in her voice.

"Almost." He checked the saddlebags. Everything was ready. "I want you to put your arms around my neck."

"What?"

"Do as I say."

Annabeth didn't argue. Lowering himself, Ransom reached behind and gathered her legs under the crook of his arms. Annabeth let out a cry of surprise. Taking the horses' reins in the other hand, he walked into the cave. The light slowly faded, and Annabeth suddenly struggled free from his grasp.

"There should be a torch around here somewhere," she said, walking to the wall. "Here it is. Now, can I have some flint and steel, since you took mine with my sword belt?"

In a minute, Ransom struck the steel and flint together, sparking the torch to life.

"You aren't going to let me do a thing, are you?"

"Someone has to look after you," he said with a smile.

"It's not far, and it is only one torch. I can manage that."

"Fine," he said, handing her the torch and then slipping an arm around her. "But you are not going to walk *all* by yourself."

When they came into the light again, Annabeth sagged down onto the grass.

Ransom sat down beside her, letting the horses feed on the mountain grass.

"Why are you helping me?" she asked in a whisper, turning towards him.

Ransom settled himself back on his elbow in the grass, watching a butterfly land on some nearby flowers. When it floated away with the breeze, he turned to Annabeth, who hadn't taken her eyes off of him.

"Why do you want to know?"

"I have never met someone who has helped me out of the goodness of their heart before."

"And you don't believe it is possible."

"Not if you are willing to kill."

"Annabeth, you have to understand the sword is the only thing I am good at doing. I like the excitement and adventure."

She looked at him skeptically.

"You don't believe me?"

Sighing, Annabeth looked up into the sky, avoiding answering his question.

"Who is Alf?"

Annabeth changed colors before becoming cryptically silent. "What makes you think I know anyone named Alf?"

"You called me Alf when you were ill."

"I was ill?"

"Delirious with fever, in fact."

She was silent, her lips tightening as she gazed into the distance.

"You don't remember, do you?"

Annabeth changed the subject abruptly. "The cottage isn't far from here. If you don't mind, I would like to try riding by myself."

"Not at all," he said, rising and pulling Annabeth to her feet. In a moment, he scooped her into his arms and onto her saddle.

A flush reddened her cheek.

"You didn't think I would let you do all that work now, did you?"

Annabeth didn't reply, but let her eyes sweep the landscape around and below them.

Ransom mounted and she tapped her horse's sides, urging them into a small wood, then up the mountain and around to a small cottage with a shed beside it.

Riding into the shed, Annabeth dismounted and leaned against her horse, petting his neck as if nothing was the matter.

"Annabeth, why don't you go inside? I can put the horses up," said Ransom, coming beside her.

"I am good," she said, moving to the side of her horse and undoing the saddle girth.

"Annabeth." Ransom touched her waist, avoiding her wound. "You need to save your strength if you are going to get any better."

She turned to him.

"I am fine."

"Are you really?"

Something in his voice and eyes made her quiver inside. Annabeth lost her words. Turning to sort out the strange feeling, she grazed her wound roughly against his hand and winced, pausing in her turn. In that moment he gently applied his hand against her waist far away from the wound and began leading her out of the shed.

Annabeth felt his sheathed dagger handle brush against her arm. She pulled the dagger from his belt. He paused at her swift motion. Turning fully to face him, she put the dagger's tip against his throat.

"Why are you helping me?"

Ransom stepped away, but Annabeth followed until he was against the wall, the tip still laid at his throat.

Ransom looked into her eyes. She was weak. He could easily take the dagger from her hand, strike a fist into her wounded side, and conquer her, but it wasn't his way.

"Why?" Her eyes became level and touched with cold; she was ready for whatever would come.

Ransom let out a sigh. "I was hired to come find

you."

The tip pressured dangerously at his jugular, ready to pierce it and send him to his grave.

"By whom?" her voice was calm.

"King Fredric."

"What?" she looked at him, taken aback, the tip releasing its sharp taste. A moment later she recovered herself. "You are lying."

"He sent me to fetch you, to keep you safe."

Annabeth shook her head, leaning the point deeper into his neck. "No. You are lying."

"It is so, Annabeth." He looked into her eyes, feeling no fear or dread. "Your father saved his life on the battlefield when King Fredric and he fought side by side for the Holy Lands. He remembered your father's name, and when he heard that you, his daughter, were in distress, he sent me to fetch you into his court. Telling me to '*Find her, earn her trust, and bring her to me, for her father's sake.*'"

"I don't believe you."

"You don't have to. But it is the truth."

Annabeth looked into his eyes, searching them with questions filling her own. She pressed the dagger harder against his throat.

Ransom closed his eyes. If he hadn't earned her

trust by now, he was never going to. It was better to die failing his mission than to live and fail.

"Why did King Fredric want to save me?"

"For your father's sake," he repeated without opening his eyes.

"Why? Why would he want to save me?"

Ransom opened his eyes and let them pierce into hers. "He said something about the brotherhood of the body of Christ."

Her mouth quivered. Turning, she stepped away. Ransom stood where he was.

Taking a deep breath, she looked up to the sky. Releasing the air, she squared her shoulders and turned back to him.

"If you are lying to me, I *will* take your life."

"Why should I lie to you?"

The question baffled her and she looked at him, her brow wrinkling.

He came to her side, brushing back a stray hair from her face before dropping his hands to his side and looking down into her eyes.

"Annabeth, I want to be your friend. Can you believe that?"

She looked challengingly into his eyes. "How much is he paying you to be my friend?"

"I am his personal spy and soldier. He paid me to bring you to him, not to be your friend. He said if you didn't cooperate I was to tie you up, gag you, and drag you across the border. But considering everything, I would rather you came of your own will."

With a toss of her chin Annabeth looked over her shoulder, away from him into the valley.

"You don't have to trust me. You don't have to believe me. It's all up to you."

"And if I say yes?"

"I would be honored to be your friend."

"And if I say no?"

"I would rather you just killed me on the spot."

Annabeth stepped away from him, startled by his words. "Why?"

Ransom just shook his head. "I am not afraid of death. Why should I care?"

She shook her head and looked up into his face. "All right."

His eyes asked her where they stood.

Taking the dagger, she laid it in his hand.

"I'll trust you for *now*." Her emphasis was soft, but still it held the entire right to withdraw her opinion.

Ransom couldn't help but notice that she had grown paler the longer they talked. He feared the damage that might come to her, but he did not dare rush things. As she walked past him, her body trembled and she started to collapse. Catching her mid-fall, he lifted her into his arms and carried her into the small cottage. Laying her on the cot, he quietly went about restoring her.

When Annabeth came to, her eyes met his calmly. They were fearless and off guard. She was exhausted.

She trusted him.

"I am going to look at your wound, all right? It's going to hurt, but I have to make sure that you are fine."

Nodding, she gathered the blanket in her fists, ready for what pain would come.

Taking away the bandage, he cleaned around the wound and bound it up again.

"Close your eyes and get some sleep. I'll go tend to the horses. All you have to do is call if you need anything."

Wearily, she nodded. He watched as her body sagged against the bed, relaxing completely. Her eyes fluttered shut, and her breathing slowed into a steady rhythm.

CHAPTER 8

Annabeth didn't wake from her slumber until the next morning. Ransom kept a close eye on her throughout the night, waking every hour or so to make sure she was not falling into a fever or any worse malady.

Ransom turned around from placing bannock next to the fire to find Annabeth watching him.

"Good morning."

"Morning." Her eyes flitted around the cottage.

Rising, he went to her side and gently touched her forehead. "How did you sleep?"

"Like the dead."

Ransom chuckled. "I am glad to see you are still with us, then."

"Are there signs of anyone?"

Ransom shook his head. "Not a one."

"Have you even been outside?"

"I fed the horses and walked around the perimeter and down the trail, all the way to the cave, and back another way, dropping around from the back."

Annabeth looked satisfied.

The day passed quietly as they both caught up on lost sleep. Ransom was content to sleep in front of the fireplace. As the stars came out, he woke to the sound of the cot creaking loudly. Annabeth had her legs over the side and pushed herself to stand.

"What exactly do you think you are doing?"

She started and turned to him. "I didn't think you were awake."

"I wasn't, but I am now," he said dryly.

"I am sorry. I didn't mean to wake you. I have to move or I will become stiff all over."

"You will lie back on that cot and save your strength."

"Ransom, I just can't." She moved towards the door of the cottage.

He looked at her. It was the first time she had used his name.

"Annabeth."

She kept going towards the door. Upon opening it, she leaned against the doorframe. The moonlight fell on her, softening everything about her, even the bloodstain on her dress.

Rising, he went to the door and leaned on the other side of the frame, crossing his arms and resting one foot behind the other on the tip of his boot. He waited in silence.

"I can't go with you," she whispered.

He didn't react, but glanced at her sideways.

Annabeth looked up at him. It was obvious by the look in her eye she was steadfast. "I am not going with you."

"Why not?"

"You wouldn't understand."

"Try me."

Leaning further into the doorway, she rested her head against the frame and looked out and away from him.

"I can't leave my father there."

"You don't know if he is alive or dead."

"I won't leave him or the people. They depend on me. So much depends on me," she said, sighing and squaring her shoulders.

"How do the people depend on you?"

"Have you ever heard the talk about me?"

"A little here and there."

"I once heard a woman say that if I ever got captured she knew 'we would all be dun fur by Lord Rabun.'"

Ransom smiled at the way she broke into the peasant way of speech.

"That is only one woman, Annabeth, and leaving isn't being captured."

"But what can I do in your country? How will your king help my people? They need me here, if nothing else, to keep Lord Raburn and his men from plaguing them all to pieces."

"Annabeth."

"It's true. You don't know him like I do."

"And how well do you know him?"

"I was brought up in his house. My father was his captain of the guard. The king often hired his services, for he was a very skilled swordsman, but my father was bound to Raburn by an oath of loyalty and brotherhood that he would not break..." her words fell off into a sigh. She pushed herself away from the door, muttering under her breath. "I am tired."

Walking across the room, she laid down gingerly on the cot and turned her back to him. Ransom walked out the door, closing it behind him; he tended the horses. When he came back in, Annabeth was sleeping.

The next few days passed quietly. He did not press her for her mysteries; he would wait until she could not hold them. He spent many of his spare hours keeping the horse tack in shape, mending the wear and tear, making up their supply of flour into bannock, getting water from the nearby stream, and making sure they weren't followed or found. This left Annabeth to memorize the cracks in the ceiling and the knotholes in the rafters and count away the hours. She was growing restless. Something was eating at her.

They had been at the cottage almost a week when Ransom awoke to find her cot empty and the door ajar. Jumping to his feet, he slid into the darkness.

Annabeth was in the shed saddling her horse.

Ransom laid his hand on the horse's back. "Were you going to tell me?"

Biting her lower lip, she tightened the saddle girth and moved away to put on the horse's bridle.

"Annabeth."

She turned to face him. "I told you I can't go with you."

"I know you told me that, but it still doesn't make any sense."

"Of course it doesn't. You aren't in my position; you don't have a price on your head; you don't have a father locked in dungeon; you don't have a—" she stopped short. "You have to let me go. When it is all over, I will come with you. But I can't leave. I won't. Not until I know it is all over."

Slowly, he stepped forward, his arms bridging the

gap between the horses.

"The more I know, the better. How can I help you if you don't allow me to know all of the details? I need to know everything."

"My favorite color is blue," she said flippantly.

Ransom smiled. "I meant all the details of the price on your head."

Annabeth smiled for a moment, then became serious and silent. Taking a deep breath, she opened her mouth and closed it. It was too difficult to speak about just at that moment. Annabeth took the reins of her horse and started to back him out of the stable.

"Where do you think you are going?"

"I already told you I am not going with you, and I can't stay here any longer. I can't, Ransom, I just can't."

"Can you at least tell me why you have to go? I can't understand unless you tell me."

For a long time, there was silence. Annabeth couldn't seem to face the words and let them out of her heart, so Ransom opened the conversation.

"I hear Lord Raburn is a very reasonable man. Why is he being so unreasonable about you?"

She shook her head in a frustrated manner. "Everyone says he is reasonable because they are afraid of him. No one dares cross him, because if they do he will double cross them twice as hard, and sink every hope they ever laid eyes on."

"That isn't a compliment."

"It's the truth," she said, trying to face her own words. She turned to him. "He wants me so he can break me and my father and destroy the kingdom."

"Your father?"

"Yes, my father is—was Lord Raburn's captain of the guard. My father is—was—is—I don't know if he is dead or alive. He is a professional soldier, and the best sword master I have ever seen. You can imagine what a disappointment it was for him to have a girl."

Annabeth turned away, walking to the end of the shed. She leaned against the hay rack.

"What kind of man is your father?"

"He is the kind of man who…who is my father" Annabeth answered vaguely.

Ransom looked at her curiously, trying to pry into her heart and understand.

Annabeth sighed in frustration. "I don't know how to explain it to you. I never thought I could love someone like I loved my mother. I always failed him; I was a girl; but when he came home from the war he was different."

"War changes men."

"I am talking about a good different. For the first time in my whole life, I felt that he loved me. Then I had to go and spoil it all and run away like a coward, and I keep running because I am too much of a fool to stop." Her voice was choked with tears, but she held it back as one who had nearly mastered the art.

He stepped closer, leaning sideways so he could see her face. "Do you ever cry?"

"What is the use of tears? I will only feel worn out when it is all done," she answered bitterly.

"Sometimes I find tears relieve the feelings, especially in the tender heart of a girl. A girl like you could do with a good cry."

"You aren't afraid of my tears?" she asked, trying to laugh.

"Why would I be? They are only salty drops of water filled with emotion, passion, and grief."

She smirked, tossing her head with a slight huff and turned away. "You speak nonsense."

"Do I?"

"Of course you do."

He stepped in front of her. "Be yourself. It's all right to cry, you know."

"Crying makes people weak," she said, trying to push past him, but there he still stood.

"Who says?"

"It's a common fact."

"Self-pity makes one weak, not tears."

"What is that you want from me?"

"I want you to be yourself. I want you to let go of whatever is holding you back."

"And if I fall apart and am too weak to continue on? What then?"

"I will look out for you."

"And when you are gone?"

"I won't leave you."

"People always leave me—my mother and now my father. You are going to go, too. I know it. I can feel it here," she said, touching her heart.

"Then I promise, if I ever leave you, I will always return. I will never leave you completely alone."

"That's not possible. You are human, and humans change."

"I will not change, Annabeth."

"You will; everybody does. It is human nature to change."

"Then I will change for the better."

Annabeth pushed past him, grabbing her horse's reins. "You don't know what you are talking about."

Ransom closed his hand over Annabeth's, halting

her retreat.

"Tell me."

"No. I can't. You have no idea who I am or what I am doing. This is my fight—my war. Stay out of it."

"No. I won't. Why is Lord Raburn after you?"

She shook her head. "Secrets are my only weapon. I am not about to give them up to you."

"So you have something on Raburn?"

"Maybe."

There was a long silence.

"One question before you go. Where did you learn to tie someone up like that?"

Annabeth looked up at him curiously. "The way I tied you up?"

"That is the general idea," he said, a hot feeling rushing up his neck uncomfortably.

She turned away from him, talking to the thin air in front of her. "When your father trains young men how to fight, and then trains you, too, you learn a lot of things. Especially if they catch you and make you their victim when your father isn't around."

"Did they get into trouble for it?"

"No." Annabeth sighed. "Not until Prince Alfred came along. Then they watched their manners. He was the only one who ever treated me like a lady, other than…"

"Other than who?"

Annabeth sighed. "It's not really important."

"Are you holding back on me?"

"It's not something you need to know. You don't need to know any of it, really."

"Annabeth, listen to me," he said, taking her shoulders and turning her to look him in the eye. "I am not letting you do this alone."

She tried to step away from him, but he held her fast.

"What about your king?"

"I am here to protect you."

"I might tie you up again."

"You are going to have to catch me sleeping first," he laughed.

"That shouldn't be too hard."

"You just think that. So, will you let me?"

"Do I have a choice?"

He didn't answer her question but looked into her eyes.

Annabeth's gaze dropped. "All right. I have to meet a friend; he has some information I want, and I have something for him. We have to go south."

"But you just came from there."

"I have a disguise."

"A boy again?"

"No, I have worn that one clear through. I have something a little more clever. I don't think even you will recognize me."

"Oh, I doubt that."

"We'll see."

"So, you want to leave tonight?"

"The sooner the better."

"Won't it be difficult to see in the cave?"

"We aren't going through the cave, and there is enough moonlight to see where we will be going."

CHAPTER 9

It was dark when Ransom saddled his horse and retrieved the few supplies they would need.

When he came out, Annabeth had mounted and was waiting for him. He mounted and she looked at him curiously.

"You sure you don't mind?"

"I don't. Why?"

"Just, some men I know…" She shook her head and put her heels into her horse's sides. Ransom followed.

They traveled around the mountain into a valley and out into a thick forest where the moon could barely pierce through the branches to show them the way. The sun rose as they reached the edge of the forest.

Annabeth smiled. "We made better time than I thought. We are going to have to stop here for about a half-hour while I get into my disguise. Anything beyond here is dangerous for me."

"What do you want me to do?"

"Anything you like. Just don't follow me."

He looked at her questioningly.

"I promise I shan't run away, and if I take more than a half-hour you can follow after me."

Ransom shook his head and dismounted, unsaddled, and unbridled his horse, turning him out to pasture.

He watched the sun rise and counted time pensively. Was it a good decision to take her at her word? *What if?*

As it came to the half-hour, Ransom whistled to his horse. Saddling him once more, he prepared to go after Annabeth.

Just as he finished, there was the squeaking and rattle of a rickety old cart, filled with a few belongings: a stick or two of furniture, a pile of hay, and small barrels of food. He glanced at it, only to do a double-take. It was an old lady, bent and crooked, leading a horse with mange. He had seen them before, hadn't he? There was no way in the world…was it possible?

Leading his horse towards the elderly lady, he looked at her curiously, searching for similarities.

"What are you looking at?" snapped the old woman, but with a definitely younger voice that was trying not to laugh.

"Annabeth?"

The old woman straightened, raising her stout

stick as if to thrash him. He put his hand out to block the blow.

A girlish laugh broke from the old woman.

"I said you wouldn't recognize me." Her bright eyes snapped with pleasure.

"I did recognize you."

"Only because you were looking for me. And you remembered, didn't you?"

"That I did. I can't believe I didn't see it before. But how?"

"They haven't unraveled this one yet because I pretended to be a mute, and they usually don't even stop to talk to me. So, what do you say?"

"I think it is very clever, but to be limited to a walking pace will slow you down considerably."

"Not quite. I was thinking that you could be, um…" She laughed and blushed even beneath the face powder she had used to make herself look older.

"That I could…?"

"Be escorting an elderly relative to your home or something like that."

"Ah-ha."

"I could sit on the back of the cart and you could ride and lead your horse, keeping our pace pretty strong."

He laughed. "You think of everything, don't you?"

"I have to."

"Well, let's get on the road."

"Not quite yet; I think you should be warned there is a reward on your head."

"What?"

"I don't know how they have found out, but I pulled this down a few towns ago." She retrieved the sheet of paper from the cart.

He took it and read: "Reward: five hundred pieces of gold for the man assisting Annabeth. Be ye warned they are armed and dangerous..."

Annabeth pulled the paper from his hands. "People will make up such nonsense these days."

She slid the paper back into the haystack, pulled out an old leather jerkin and gray workman's shirt, and offered them to him.

"There is no description, but just in case."

"Anything that fits you I doubt will fit me."

"They are too big for me; they should fit well."

Ransom began to take off his leather jerkin and shirt. Annabeth turned away and walked to the end of the cart. Looking up at the sun, she shielded her eyes.

When he had finished, Ransom came to her side. "Where do I put these?"

"Oh," she said, and pulled out a sack, putting the clothes in. She slipped them under the hay.

"To pull off the whole farmer look, you might want to put your sword under the hay."

"Is that where yours is?"

She nodded. "They have never looked there before, and it keeps me safe. I mean, an old woman with a sword looks rather suspicious."

Ransom laughed. "How did you know these would fit me?"

"Just a wild guess. I picked them up a long time ago. I thought I would trim them down to my size. Just never got the time, I guess," she said with a shrug of her shoulders. "Shall we?"

Ransom nodded. "I think that would be a good plan." He looked at her archly, and added dryly, "Grandmother."

Annabeth burst out laughing. "Don't call me that or I shall not keep a straight face."

Gently picking up Annabeth, he sat her on the stack of hay. "There; now you can rest, and not strain yourself."

"Ransom, I…"

"You are still wounded and need all of your strength."

"I can manage just fine."

"You will lie there and rest, or I'll tie you to the cart."

"You wouldn't dare!"

"Don't try me."

She leaned against the hay, her eyes trying to sift him out. He didn't give her that chance, but, mounting, took the horse's bridle and began to lead the rickety old cart onto the road and head south.

CHAPTER 10

Three days later, Annabeth said it was time to stop and make camp in the middle of the day.

"We'll stop here until midday tomorrow. If he doesn't show up by then, it is time to move on."

After they made camp, Annabeth slipped behind a bush and pulled out a carefully wrapped package. Opening it, she smiled. "It's still here."

Ransom looked over at her, asking with his eyes.

"A new dress—or rather an old dress, but it will feel new after these rags."

She took off her neat little white cap and shook her head vigorously, letting her hair fall loosely about her as a cloud of flour surrounded her. Coughing, she walked away from the cloud. Her fingers still came away powdered as she ran them through her hair. She shivered, looking something like a little bird that had just hopped out of a dust bath and was trying to adjust her feathers properly again.

"Would you mind if I went down to the river to wash this off?" she said, rubbing her face and wiping away some of the wrinkles.

"Don't mind one bit. I'll be here unless you call."

"Thank you," she said, gathering her skirts up and dashing away.

Within half an hour she returned, wearing a faded blue dress and carrying damp clothes gingerly over one arm; her wet hair was loosely braided and over her shoulder.

She spread the washed clothes out on a low branch to dry and sat down before the small fire that Ransom had started. He was whittling the end of a long stick.

"Do you know how to spear a fish?" he asked casually.

Across the flame, she met his eyes. There seemed to be unexpected dampness in them. "I do."

"What do you say about some fresh fish for our dinner?"

"It sounds splendid."

"Then this one is yours." He tossed the stick lengthwise over the fire.

She caught it with a single hand and looked at the sharp tip. "It's a good one."

Rising, he started towards the river, carrying his own.

At the riverbank, they took off their knee-high boots and slipped into the water. Ransom headed towards a deep, clear pool; Annabeth hopped nimbly from one moss-covered stone to the next until she reached a shallow where the water ran swiftly.

In a minute, Ransom had stabbed a fish from the water and tossed it onto the bank. Two more came in quick succession before Annabeth made her first stab into the water, coming up empty.

Ransom glanced in her direction.

"I said I could. I didn't say I was good."

He only smiled and shook his head.

Her next stab was successful.

Ransom came up with three more fish and called it a successful expedition. Together they skinned the fish, then cooked them over the open fire.

Annabeth was strangely mute during the whole process, her eyes saying that her mind was occupied as she mechanically turned the fish over and over on the spit.

Several times she shook her head as if trying to shake something out of her mind, then glanced thoroughly around the forest, all the while turning the spit. Ransom laid his hand over hers to take his turn, and she jumped with a sharp intake.

"What's the matter?"

"Nothing," she answered with a shake of her head.

"I hope I should know you a little better than that."

"Fine, something is, but I am not in the mood to talk about it." Going to the old cart, she pulled out her sword and fastened it around her waist with a slight wince–the belt rested against her wound.

Ransom watched her with scrutinizing eyes. She checked the dampness of her clothes, walked the perimeter of the camp, climbed a tree with low branches for a better view before walking around again. By that time, the fish were done and he called her to eat.

"Is something wrong?"

"No, just my nerves."

He nodded and served up the fish. He watched as she silently cut a piece and took a bite, chewing slowly. She couldn't seem to swallow. Taking a sip from her canteen, she suddenly stood up.

"I'll be back in a little while."

Ransom watched her disappear and gave her a few minutes before following. She was sitting by the river, tossing in pebbles, her knees hugged against her. He sank down beside her, watching her and the river.

She threw another pebble before gathering her

knees more tightly into her chest. Holding them with both arms, she rested her chin on one knee.

"The last day I had with my father, we went fishing together. He…" She sighed and bit her lip, trying to find the words she needed.

"It was the day he told me everything that had happened to him in the Holy Land. How he and King Harold were both captured together; how he had no hope but in himself; and how all of his attempts at escape were useless. King Harold was different from any other man he had known. He didn't fight, but he was strong, he was not fearful, and he never gave up believing that all would be well even after they were sentenced to death. It is hard to imagine my father fearful, but he was afraid of death. Then when King Harold shared his faith and my father believed, he said that it felt as if a lightning bolt came down from heaven, and he saw a way of escape. He felt that it was his chance to come back to me, and be the father he needed to be."

She looked out at the stream, her eyes blind to what was before her as memories floated in her mind.

"My mother was one of the faith, and she passed it on to me. She died in childbirth when I was eight. The baby was a boy, and he died only days later. My father felt thwarted and angry at God and forbade me to believe or pray. I didn't openly, but I begged God every day to give me a father who would love me. I tried everything I could think of to make him love me. I became his son; I fought; I battled; I wanted his love more than anything. I prayed for years, and then when God finally gave it to me I gave it all away. I told my father everything that had happened in his absence.

"He was so calm. He rose to his feet, told me to stay there, and said if he wasn't back within the hour to ride like the wind. I waited for him. It was over an hour but I couldn't bear the thought of just leaving, so I waited. I waited until I heard the hounds. Then I fled, and I have been doing that ever since. But still God has been good to me," she said, dropping her eyes to the ground.

"How can you say that?"

"Some things look awful; other things look beautiful. Whatever His purpose, I know they are perfect. My mother's death was sad and I was left alone, but because of my grief, I came closer to God. Because my father was captured, his life was changed forever. He came back a father; a man I admire and love. God has even sent you to protect me. I don't know what God is doing now, Ransom, because I can't see the whole plan; all I see is my little world. Does it frighten me? Yes, it does. But He has taken care of me in the past, and I know He will take care of the future. He knows when each sparrow falls, and the hairs on my head; He will not forget me, Ransom. I know *He will not*."

Ransom looked into her blue eyes. They were almost filled with tears, so earnest. He searched those eyes looking up into his for anything that would betray the way she really felt. There was nothing; she honestly felt that way with all her heart.

Ransom slipped his arm around her shoulders. Closing her eyes, she leaned her head against his shoulder, letting out a sigh of weariness.

I will protect her always, he promised in his heart.

"Do you think you could eat something now? You need to keep up your strength."

"I think I could manage it."

Rising, he took her hands, pulling Annabeth to her feet.

Chapter 11

The day passed slowly. Ransom returned to the river to fish for dinner while Annabeth elected to stay back at camp to keep the fire burning and watch for her friend. When Ransom returned an hour later with the fish cleaned and ready to eat, Annabeth was waiting, the fire in the state of perfection, with a surprise. She had made a basket out of fresh leaves and sharp twigs. In the little basket were cradled late berries.

"Where did you find those?" Ransom asked, snatching one up and popping it into his mouth.

"Not far from here. They are late because they grew so much in the shade, but aren't they splendid?"

Ransom took another and nodded.

"Now don't eat too many of them. I was saving them to eat *with* the fish."

Ransom watched as Annabeth put some of their food by for travel and left some close to the fire to stay warm.

"So, who is this friend we are waiting for?" Ransom asked, settling himself down and looking at her rather sleepily across the fire.

Leaning forward, Annabeth stirred the coals with a stick, sending sparks flying like dancing orange fireflies towards the sky. Distractedly, she put on another log.

Ransom sat up and leaned forward, staring at her though the fire.

Her chin was resting on her knee as she held it close, gazing into the waving flames. Their eyes met; she stared into the coals and stirred them with the stick again, and looked away into the night, waiting, watching.

"Why does Raburn want you so badly?"

"Secrets. Secrets about him he doesn't want anyone to know about. You see, I am the only one who knows them, and the moment I am dead…" She sighed and met his eyes. "He can kill Prince Alfred."

"What?"

"I know what his plans are, and what he will do, but as long as there is a threat of me telling the whole story, the prince must stay alive. For if he kills him, I will let the whole world know and he will be destroyed."

"Why not tell the whole world now?"

"And make the people more afraid and terrified of him? No, I couldn't do that. Very few of the people are armed since the king left; Raburn has seen to that. The town you first met me in is one of his greatest resisters, but they could not face an army. My hands are tied. If I tell everyone the truth, the people will be in a rage with nothing to defend themselves but their anger, and if I don't say a thing, he gets away with murder."

Ransom looked at her questioningly.

"I saw him kill Prince Alfred's lord protector. They were having a disagreement. Lord Raburn would not compromise his position, and neither would the lord protector. So, he pretended to compromise, agreed on a handshake, and then choked the man to death once he was close enough. He dragged the lord protector to his room and had the doctor swear that he died of a heart attack in his sleep. Before anyone else could see the body, there was an accidental fire that destroyed the lord protector's chambers, and the doctor died of a stroke the next day, drinking to Lord Raburn's heath as the new lord protector. You see, I am running for not only my life, but others as well. The moment I am in his grasp, he will have something new to torture my father with. Then, when we are both dead, he will kill the prince and be done with it all. No one dares to stand up to him."

"Why do you dare to stand up to him?"

Annabeth looked blankly at him. "I don't have

another choice unless I want to become one of his tools—and I don't. If he lays a finger on Prince Alfred, the whole country shall know it. I will raise them up in arms if it comes to that."

"And how is that?"

Annabeth smiled elusively as she gazed into the fire. "You might say a little birdie knows."

"The phantom Song Lark?"

Annabeth nodded with a little smile.

"I haven't heard of it singing in a while."

"The bird knows when to warble and when to be silent, just like the wild ones."

"And does that little bird happen to be close by?"

"I don't know," she said, glancing up into the trees. There was rustle in the forest and both laid hold of their swords and crept to their feet, sliding slowly away from the fire in opposite directions.

There was a strum of a lute.

"Oh, oh, I pray thee hark, and my words thy heart will spark."

Annabeth put down her sword and answered back.

"I pray thee welcome, I pray thee mark; thy name must be Song Lark."

A hearty laugh burst from the forest.

"That's a new one, Annabeth!"

"Hello, Lark."

"How is the nest?"

"It is safe and snug. It's only my friend and I."

"Ah, so you have brought your friend to meet me. I have heard about him. Raburn doesn't like him."

Annabeth laughed. "There is nothing that he does like. But allow me to introduce you. Song Lark, this is Ransom."

"It's a pleasure to meet you."

"And I, you," said Ransom, stepping forward and offering his hand.

Song Lark shook it, then thrummed his fingers over the strings of his lute with a smile at Annabeth.

"What news do you have for me to hear? What food do you have for me to eat?"

"There is fish if you want it, and a few berries."

He sat down promptly and began to eat.

Annabeth sat and waited in silence for him to be done.

"So, what news do you have, Annabeth?"

"When I was in the south, I was able to make contact with Christina's maidservant. She had a note from Prince Alfred. He doesn't think he has long. Lord Raburn is getting more irritable and threatening than usual."

"Did you hear he moved the prince up to Anondorf?"

"Anondorf?" she asked, paling.

Song Lark nodded.

"It makes sense; he has spent years fortifying the place and making it a labyrinth of death."

"Have you heard anything about your father?"

"No. I don't think he is dead yet though…but then again, he could be. It all depends on how badly he wants me to hope or die."

"If the prince is running out of time, we need to do something. There is no knowing when the king will come back, and I would like to know that his son is safe, sound, and ready to take the throne."

"But how, Lark?"

"I am not sure, but it has to be done."

"I know."

For a long time they all sat around the fire in silence: thinking, scheming, planning.

Slowly, Annabeth looked over at Song Lark, her eyes filling with hope and questions.

"Song Lark, do you have those old monk robes yet?"

"Of course I do; what else would you expect from

the master of disguise? Why, what do you want them for?"

"I was just wondering if," she smiled in her excitement. "Do you think that Ransom is about the same height as the prince?"

"What are you getting at there, you little schemer?"

"You and Ransom could go up to the prince's room to inquire about his soul and hear his prayers or something. Ransom could change clothes with the prince, and the prince could escape as the monk, and Ransom could escape out the window as the prince. When they go to check on the prince later, they will find a rope out the window and will chase Ransom and not the prince. We can agree on a place to meet, and then the prince can cross the border and be safe and..."

Annabeth paused, paling, as she realized that this action could very well seal her father's fate in death. Lord Raburn, in anger, might take his vengeance out on him...*if* he was still alive.

"Would it work?" she asked, forcing her voice not to tremble.

The men looked at her curiously.

"Ransom, stand next to Annabeth."

Both rose and faced Song Lark.

He tilted his head.

"Face each other. Annabeth, don't be shy; look up at him. Now, Ransom put your hand on her shoulder, I need to know for sure if you are tall as Prince Alfred, and that is the way I saw them together last."

Annabeth's cheeks flamed red, her dagger withdrew and she threw it in the direction of the minstrel. Her dagger sank into the log he leaned against.

"Song Lark!" she scolded.

He threw back his head and laughed. "It's true."

"I had just received word that my father had been captured and was believed to be dead."

"And he was trying to comfort you, I suppose."

"It's not like that, Song Lark, and you know it."

"I do? Then how come you are blushing red as the lovers' rose?"

Walking over, she pulled her dagger out of the log. "I should have aimed for your throat."

Song Lark laughed and eased himself down, resting his head against the log.

"Well, if we are going to go rescue the prince I suggest we get some sleep. We have a long ride ahead of us tomorrow."

"How well does the prince know you, Song Lark?"

"Well, enough I suppose, but it has been nigh on two years since I've seen him last."

"Does he know who you are, Song Lark?"

Song Lark sat up. "No, he doesn't. He hasn't even seen me since the last lord protector was killed. Lord Raburn has never taken kindly to minstrels. He needs silence to think, and we only get on his nerves. But come to think of it, how will the prince know that we aren't fooling him into being killed? He is wise enough not to jump at any chance he gets."

They looked at Annabeth.

"I can't go into that castle. Everybody knows me. I'll be in chains and in the dungeon before you can say 'God save the king.' He is trying to lure me in; why else would he put my father and the prince in the same castle? I can't go in any of my disguises; they are too thin to face Raburn directly, and I could never sneak in a monk's robe."

Song Lark sighed. "How else will he try to escape with us, Annabeth? He knows that Raburn is just waiting for him to try something. He won't come unless he knows it is your plan."

"I would take Ransom's place, but for the height difference and that he would see right through it. The man is paranoid and will notice any small change in height. Two short monks and then a short and tall one; it wouldn't work, and you have to be the one to carry off the monk part because I can't, and Ransom can't speak much so they won't try and speak to the prince and notice the difference. Ransom shall have taken some vow of silence, I suppose. But I don't see how we can get around the fact that I can't go with you."

"I think there might sneak in under a monk's robe."

"Oh, no, Song Lark, I am not…"

Song Lark smiled at her, picked the strings of his lute, and broke into song.

There was a man sentenced to death

Who by a friend's cunning lived to take many a breath.

This friend he had was very slim

Who when he heard of his plight went off to rescue him.

Hey no ne no ne hey no ne no ne

The man arrived out of breath,

He whispered, "Friend, I've come to save you from death."

"Why, you've grown so plump!"

"Is that so?" and he dropped his burden with a thump.

Hey no ne no ne hey no ne no ne
A dead man took his place,
And he disappeared without a single trace.
This is what friends are for:
To keep you far, far away from death's open door.
Hey no ne no ne hey no ne no ne

Annabeth laid her dagger against the strings as he began a second rendition of the song.

"You are a fool if you think I would attempt such a thing."

He raised his eyes coolly to hers. "I have been called many a thing, but never a fool. To be honest, I don't think you have much choice in the matter."

She looked at Ransom, seeming to plead with him to say something.

"I think it would work, Annabeth. You'll come out the window with me. The prince and a page escaping would be perfect."

"And think about the danger that will come to me when I shrink considerably after you disappeared," said Song Lark, his hand over his middle.

"Oh, we'll put a pillow in there to satisfy whatever you require," answered Annabeth sharply.

Song Lark looked over at Ransom and yawned. "Well, what do you say, my man? Will the plan work?"

Ransom thought it through. Then he nodded. "It will work perfectly, I think."

"Well then, good night," and taking his cloak, Song Lark pulled it about himself and closed his eyes.

Ransom and Annabeth exchanged glances and lay down to sleep on their respective sides of the fire that was now a mere glow.

It was the middle of the night when Ransom awoke to the sound of a quiet struggle. He sat upright, hand on his sword, ready.

His eyes ran over the camp and then he saw Annabeth tossing and turning. Her hands seemed to be trying to push something away, but she couldn't. The sounds she made were helpless sounds: hurt, wounded, afraid.

She sat upright with a gasp. The moonlight caught the sweat dripping down her face. Pulling her knees into her chest, she leaned on them, taking in deep breaths and trying to calm her fluttering nerves.

Ransom waited, unsure of what to do.

Her shoulders began to quake, not the quake of fear but of silent tears. Ransom came to her side.

"What is the matter, Annabeth?" he asked softly.

She turned away.

Ransom leaned close. "Beth?"

He gently laid his hand on her shoulder—she quivered at his touch.

Laying his hand against her face, he turned it toward him. Tears shone in her eyes.

"What am I doing, Ransom?" she asked, her voice shaking. "What am I doing?"

He felt puzzled. "What do you mean, Beth?"

"This is all my fault!" Her whole body had begun to tremble.

"Annabeth, you need to get some sleep. That is just your nerves speaking."

"I was afraid; I am afraid. I should have spoken up long ago. I can't even say some of the things I should say, so I tell them to Song Lark and he tells other people. I have no voice. I am nothing. Nothing!"

She paused, breathing hard.

Ransom opened his mouth to speak, but she continued.

"When my father left for the Holy Land with the king, I was left in the king's household as a maid. I wasn't much good at that. I am better with a sword, and the prince and I spent a lot of our time together. When the news of my father's capture and believed death reached us, Lord Raburn claimed me as his ward, and I legally was, but…I didn't want to go with him. I knew what he was, what he was capable of, what he wanted me for. He is a master of torture and death, in so many fashions." Annabeth shuddered.

"That is who he wanted me to become: his right hand in death. I fought him every step of the way when he was teaching me, so he left off my training for a lonely, locked up room until I was willing to learn. When my father returned to his service, Lord Raburn made me swear that I would not tell my father of his treatment of me in his absence. Nothing would have brought me to tell him that in a thousand years. He wouldn't have cared, anyway."

She turned to face him. "Then when he came back changed, he was different—the father I had always longed for. I burst and told him everything I had seen: the lord protector murdered, my training with Lord Raburn, and the whole scheme of his plans. If I hadn't told him, none of this would have happened. I wouldn't be running, and he wouldn't be locked up in the dungeon." At the final word, her skin broke into goosebumps and she shivered violently.

Ransom pulled his cloak over her. "Annabeth, that isn't the truth."

"Then how come it feels like it?"

"You are tired, and you've just woken up from a

bad dream."

She looked at him startled, and he met her eyes calmly. "I didn't cry out, did I?"

"No, but whatever it was, disturbed you. What was it?"

She shook her head and looked away. "I am sorry for waking you," she murmured.

"What is it, Beth?" he said, rubbing her arm to take away the chill.

She shook her head, pressing her lips together, hard. Suddenly they quivered and she turned, pressing her forehead against his shoulder, burying her face against him. He felt fear shoot through her spine and he wrapped his arms tightly around her.

Her hands gripped his doublet.

Ransom let time pass, then slowly turned so his mouth was beside her ear.

"What is it, Annabeth?"

Slowly, she pulled away from his shoulder. Laying her hands on the ground, she stared at them. "Something is wrong. I have had that dream before, but it was never this bad."

He stroked a stray piece of hair away from her face. "Something is wrong with saving the prince?"

"Not that. It's something else, but I don't know

what."

"What is the dream?"

She bit her lip and slowly raised her eyes to his. "It's—my father in Raburn's dungeon. Only, I was there with him this time."

"Oh, Beth." There was a pang in his voice and he pulled her close. "I won't let that happen."

"I know you won't, but if…" she couldn't finish the sentence. "It scares me."

"Don't let it frighten you, and try to get some rest. You will need all of your strength."

"I can never sleep after that dream."

"Just try," he said, squeezing her hand and moving so her head rested on his shoulder.

Ransom waited until he knew that she had fallen asleep before sliding her head gently onto the ground. He crept to his own place by the fire and fell asleep.

Chapter 12

Two monks sat on the seat of an old rickety cart whose left wheel squeaked considerably. Their hoods were pulled well down over their faces to block them from the hot afternoon sun. One was a tall, thin monk who had a sense of youth about him, while the other was round and as fat as an old cat that had swallowed a rat or two whole.

They rolled up to a fortress that seemed black and cold even in the middle of the day.

Looking up, the fat monk hollered, "Hello up there? Have you table and rest for two weary strangers?"

There was a murmur at the top of the wall, and slowly the drawbridge was let down and the weary little pony pulled the cart across.

A stable boy came up and took the bridle, leading the horse and cart to the edge of the courtyard.

The young monk leapt down from the cart and came around to the old monk. The man waddled over the wheel and dropped heavily to the ground.

The fall was jarring. Annabeth ground her teeth against letting out any sounds that would give away her hiding place. The rope chaffed around her wrists, the hay they had used to round out Song Lark's figure made her itch, and what was worse, she could do nothing about it. Closing her eyes, she took a deep breath and let it out slowly.

"Hello, dear brothers."

The voice made her just about turn inside out. Annabeth dug her fingernails deep into her palms and tried to think calmly.

He can't see you. He has no idea that you are here, Annabeth. Just breathe.

She synchronized her breathing with Song Lark's heavy panting so nothing would be detected.

"What can I do for you?" he asked with his most oily cordiality.

"Brother Matthew, here, and I, thought we packed enough food for our journey, but it turns out that we haven't. I was wondering if we could impose upon your kindness to give us a little food for our journey."

"Of course," said Lord Raburn with a low chuckle. "But I will do better than that. Come feast at my table, and I will make sure that we pack you enough for the rest of your journey."

Annabeth could tell he was satisfied with their answers, even if he was laughing at them.

"You are too kind to us; company will be a welcome thing. Brother Matthew there has taken a vow of silence, and I can tell you it has been a long journey."

"Is that so? Well, come this way."

Song Lark's shuffling waddle was getting to Annabeth as she rocked back and forth, slowly growing ill.

For the better part of a half hour, the men sat, exchanging stories and laughing.

Annabeth's emotions were caught between fear and utter outrage.

At long last, Song Lark dared broach the subject. "You are a good Lord Protector. I suppose the prince says his prayers every day?"

"He most certainly does."

"It is good to hear…" he let his voice drift off in a wishful manner.

"Would the good monk like to see the prince and hear his prayers?"

"Oh, that would be too much to ask!"

"I think not. I think he may even have a confession to make. I believe he loves a fair maiden."

"Really?"

"Most certainly."

"Well then, take us to him speedily. We mustn't let the prince live with a guilty conscience."

"Of course not, dear brother."

Annabeth heard a snap of fingers.

"Snatchel! Bring these two dear brothers up to the Prince's rooms at once."

"Yes, my lord," said a familiar voice. Everything was painfully familiar to her.

Sensing the direction they were headed, Annabeth guessed they were going towards the northern wing.

After what seemed like forever, there was a rattle of keys.

"The prince likes his privacy. The keys give him ample warning that he is about to be disturbed," she heard Snatchel explain away the reason he was locked up.

In a moment, the door creaked open and Snatchel announced them. "Two monks come to hear your prayers, your highness."

"Thank you, Snatchel," the young man said, trying not to sound annoyed. "Hello, Brothers."

"I am Brother Lucas, and this is Brother Matthew. He has taken a vow of silence, so no need to speak to him, but my, my, what cozy apartments. One could live quite *comfortably* here. I see why you do not wish to be disturbed."

At last he had said the secret words she had been waiting for. It was almost safe to appear. Annabeth waited pensively for the click of the lock to be certain they were alone with the prince. Song Lark shuffled forward.

"We have come to see about your prayers."

Annabeth couldn't wait a moment longer, and she began wriggling free of the ropes that had helped holder her in place

"Thank you, Brothers; you are very kind to…" Prince Alfred stopped as he watched the monk in wonder.

A moment later, Annabeth dropped to the floor. She flipped the robe off her head, her hair disheveled.

"Song Lark, next time we do this, I'll be the monk."

Song Lark muffled a laugh behind his hand.

A moment later, the prince was on his knees beside her.

"Anna?" he asked, half bewildered, half delighted.

"Hello, Alf," she said, turning her head to look at him as she untied the last knot of her imprisonment.

Suddenly the prince put his arms around her shoulders. "I knew you wouldn't fail me."

"Sorry it took so long."

"I am sorry you've had to suffer so much. Do you know anything about your father?"

She shook her head. "And yours?"

"The only news I have heard was just before my lord protector died, when Father said he was planning on staying on for a year or more yet."

She nodded. "We are here to get you out."

"What is the plan?"

"Ransom and I will go out the window, while you leave with Song Lark as a monk. Ransom, eh- Matthew has taken a vow of silence, so you mustn't speak to anyone."

"That is it?"

She nodded.

"Now say your prayers quick, and pray for a swift and careful journey," said Song Lark with a smile.

"It's all splendid and I am ready, but did you know Lady Christina is here?"

"No." Annabeth winced. Lord Raburn had probably moved her up there once he found out that she and her maids were informants for Annabeth.

"Yes."

"I don't like that Lord Raburn is putting you all together, you, Lady Christina, and my father..." The last word trailed off quietly.

"He is still alive—I have seen him."

Tears sprang to her eyes. "How is he?"

"Well enough. I'll tell you more later, all right?"

She nodded in agreement, pain and hope twisting in her heart. *Will he be alive after today?*

"Can you get word to Lady Christina to come see you?"

"No, but she usually comes here about this time of day."

"My only question is how in the world we are going to get her out. We planned for you, but not her."

Ransom cleared his throat. "Sorry for the interruption, but I believe I have an idea. She can leave the same way you came in."

Song Lark groaned. "Not again."

"You needn't worry. She is a lighter burden than me," Annabeth said softly.

"What'll we do in the meantime?" asked Ransom.

"Pray. Ransom, get ready to take off your robe should the keys rattle, and Annabeth, you go stand in the corner. They'll not see you there right away," said Song Lark, leading them to the far side of the room and kneeling.

There was a rattle in the lock. Ransom took off his robe and helped the prince put it on, while Song Lark stuffed a pillow up his tunic and kept on praying. The door shut almost as soon as it was open, and the keys turned in the lock. There was a rustle of soft, rich fabric. Mentally, Annabeth could feel the touch of it against her skin. It had been a long time since she had worn a pretty dress.

"Your highness?"

The prince flung back the monk's hood.

"It's you, Christina," he said, rising to his feet and coming to her side. "I was hoping you would come as faithfully as ever. We are saved."

"Do you know these men?" she asked suspiciously, resting her hands on his forearms as they came up to hold her hands.

"No, but Anna does."

"But how do you know—"

"Hello, Christina," said Annabeth shyly from her corner.

The girl turned in hopeful shock and flung her arms around her friend's neck. Tears came to her eyes, and she began to cry softly. "We are saved; we are saved at last. I knew you couldn't fail us. Oh, Anna!"

"I am so glad to see you again—but we must work quickly if we are to leave before he grows suspicious." She blinked away the dampness that had risen in her eyes.

"Of course."

"These are our friends, Song Lark and Ransom."

"Hello," she greeted with a small smile and a nod.

"There is one thing, though. You can't escape wearing that dress."

"Why not?"

"The way you have to hide, no ladies' clothes would do, and with that long train in your skirt, Song Lark would be bound to trip over it. Do you have anything we could borrow, Alf?"

"Give me a moment," he said, kneeling at the large chest at the end of his bed.

"Song Lark, give me a hand," said Ransom, stripping back the bed.

"What on earth are you doing?" asked Song Lark as he watched Ransom unwind the coil of strong silk rope they had hidden about his waist and began tying the sheets to it.

"Exactly what you think I am doing—now give me a hand."

Christina had paled at Annabeth's words.

"Anna, I can't wear *his* clothes!"

"Well, you won't get out of here alive wearing that," she said, pointing to the dress.

"I can't do it. *I won't*," she whispered.

"If *his* clothes are a problem, would you rather wear mine?"

The girl blushed modestly. "I—I'd rather just…"

"It's not an option, Christina."

"I think I would feel more comfortable in something you have worn rather than his, and he is so much bigger than either of us. I do believe you are just a little taller than me."

"I am *sure* it is the case," said Annabeth, looking *up* slightly at Christina.

"Here, Anna," said the prince, handing her an armful of clothes.

In a moment, the rope was strung across the room and the chamber was segregated. Ransom changed into princely attire while Alf finished his monk disguise. Quickly, Annabeth set to work, and in few minutes, when they said they were ready, Christina appeared, blushing, shy, and awkward in Annabeth's boy attire.

"Song Lark, start hiding her, I'll be out in a moment," Annabeth commanded from behind the curtain.

She appeared a few moments later, looking like a boy with a great ambition of growing very tall, very soon. Ransom couldn't help a smile, but immediately took down the rope and freed the sheets from it. The monks were now ready to leave.

Annabeth caught Prince Alfred's sleeve just as they were about to ask for dismissal. "Remember you have taken a vow of silence. Do not betray it."

He nodded his head, and she slipped into the corner as they knocked for dismissal.

The moment they were gone, Ransom was securing the rope to the bedpost. They waited. They had to give them time to get away in case they were caught going down the wall.

Quietly, Annabeth put the rooms to rights, then picked up Christina's dress. The fabric was soft and cool to her touch. She bit her lower lip in wishful thinking.

"You'd be pretty in a dress like that, Beth," Ransom said softly.

Annabeth felt her cheek flush as she realized he had been watching her every move intently, his arms resting confidently on his hips. He looked commanding in the prince's clothing.

"Who gave you permission to call me Beth?" she

accused, trying to find fault with him somewhere.

He smiled and almost swaggered towards her, pursing his mouth.

"Nobody," he admitted.

Then he looked down into her eyes.

"Do you mind it? Or would you rather I called you Anna?"

"I don't mind it, I guess. Anna is rather a childish pet name they have for me," she said, walking to the window and looking down.

"Oh, no," she moaned with disappointed anguish.

"What?"

"I should have known he would be paranoid enough to fill the moat. What are we going to do? I can't swim."

"No fear. You can climb down the rope?"

She nodded. "I wouldn't be up here if I couldn't."

"You are going to go down first, and hold on to the castle wall when you get down there. When I come, you will lay back and I will tow you to the far shore. All right?"

"Are you sure?"

"I am not leaving you up here to face that man's wrath." He tore part of the sheet, put it around Annabeth's waist, and tied it to the end of the rope.

"There. Now, you first just in case we get caught."

Nimbly she climbed out the window and scaled down the stone wall. As her feet touched the water in the moat, she shuddered and slowly lowered herself into it. Finding a hold in the wall with one hand, she tried to undo the knot so Ransom could pull it up again. But there was no untangling it. A moment later, the rope became taut as he slid down.

A cry of surprise and rage came from the wall, an arrow shot from a bow, it missed it's intended target but caught the rope fraying it above their heads. It quickly began to unravel, threatening to snap and send Ransom plunging into the water.

Annabeth began to pray.

Oh, God, keep us all safe and unharmed.

Before the rope could fail, he lowered himself into the water beside her.

"I can't get this knot undone," she whispered frantically.

"It's not supposed to come undone," he answered, taking his dagger from his belt. Ransom swam behind her, putting an arm over her shoulder, across her body to her waist.

"When I cut the rope, you just need to relax and breathe. I am going to pull you across."

She nodded and in a moment she was completely wet as he severed the rope. Annabeth tried to lie perfectly still as Ransom pulled her across the moat and onto the bank.

Arrows surrounded them like hail.

Once they reached shallow water, they were on their feet. They ran onto the bank and slipped into some undergrowth.

"Now for the dangerous part—running out in the open. You ready?" he asked, panting.

"Ready," Annabeth replied. Her eyes lit with enthusiasm.

They made a mad dash for the forest a good hundred yards away, where they had hidden their horses.

Arrows whizzed by them, tearing at them, barely missing.

Suddenly, Annabeth laughed, threw back her head, and started running harder.

They looked back at the castle. In the far off distance, they could see a horse cart ricketing its way into the forest. They had waited long enough. Once in the forest, there were horses. They'd be off in a moment. Mounting, they swiftly headed deep into the forest at a gallop.

Ransom watched as Annabeth rode low and close to the neck of her horse. She could not wait to be gone from this place.

In a short while, their trail was being hotly pursued by men from Raburn's castle. Arrows were darting into the forest, barely missing them as they sunk into trees and whizzed by them at a hair's breadth.

Suddenly Annabeth found herself flying over her horse's neck as he floundered into a deep hare hole. She screamed as he fell to the ground. Her mind swooned as the world seemed to dance wildly around her.

Annabeth was raising herself to her feet as Ransom came back to her. With no time for ceremony, he grabbed her by the waist and pulled her before him in the saddle.

In a moment they were making up lost ground.

The chase was long, and before it ended the horse was white with sweat, but Raburn's men were nowhere in sight.

Ransom pulled the horse to a walk and slid to the ground, taking the bridle.

"The poor creature needs a break."

Annabeth made a move to get to the ground.

His hand stayed her.

"You've had a nasty fall, and until I know how

you are I'm not letting you move."

"Can I breathe?"

"I suppose I can allow that," Ransom sighed, not seeming to hear her attempt at humor.

Annabeth fell into silence, watching with care for any sound or movement that would mean they were being followed. Long after dark, they settled down for camp without a fire. Ransom turned to help Annabeth down from the saddle, but she slipped down before he could even offer both his hands.

"How are you feeling?" Ransom asked with a slight disapproving frown.

"Well enough," Annabeth answered with a sigh; she didn't want to be bothered.

His hand touched her side. Surprised at the sudden pain his gentle touch caused her, she winced.

"Did I hurt you?"

"Just a little."

"How is your wound?"

The tenderness in his voice made her head feel like it was spinning.

"Well enough. I have been tending to it, just the fall…I think it bruised me there."

His eyes searched hers.

"You'd tell me if it was worse?"

"I think so." Suddenly Annabeth didn't feel as if she even knew her own mind. Something in his eyes confused her.

Ransom let her slip past him and sink wearily to the ground.

"That went well," she sighed.

Ransom couldn't help but laugh. "I can't imagine what your definition of bad is."

Annabeth giggled at the prospect, then sobered.

"I think that would have been having Lord Raburn walking in and arresting all of us. He would have been so happy; all of his troubles would have been over in one fell swoop: Song Lark, you, Alf, and me. Christina would have been an unfortunate witness that would have been added to the casualty list, and my father. Then it would all have been over for him. I just hope they are all right."

"They had enough horses once they were out of sight to get away with all speed."

"Christina has never been out of castle walls. I just hope she doesn't mind roughing it, and in boy's clothes, nonetheless."

"I am sure she'll find some way to manage."

"I hope so," Annabeth sighed and, laying down, closed her eyes, pulling the cloak fully around her.

"Those clothes you gave me were for the prince, weren't they?"

"Hmm?" she said, opening her eyes wearily.

"The clothes you gave me before we went to meet with Song Lark. You said I should look like a farmer. You had those laid aside for the prince, didn't you?"

"What would make you think that?"

"These fit the same way those do."

"That's good to know," Annabeth said dryly, and rolled over.

"You aren't going to answer my question, are you?"

"I don't think it needs answering," she replied shortly.

"Good night, Annabeth," he said, pulling his cloak about him and falling wearily to the ground, murmuring in his mind. "*Only a few hours...a few hours.*"

Annabeth's quiet voice broke the stillness as she turned to face him.

"They were for the prince, but it makes no matter."

Ransom caught her eyes. They were quiet, tired,

and something else he could not discern.

"Your father's going to be all right," he whispered confidently, feeling that it was so.

"Good night," she whispered, and turned over once again.

CHAPTER 13

Before dawn could stretch its first rays into the sky, Ransom and Annabeth were once again traveling.

Annabeth still rode in front of Ransom as they kept up a fast pace, but neither spoke—there was too much at stake. As the afternoon grew late, Ransom became restless and broke the silence.

"Why did you laugh yesterday?"

"When?"

"When you were running."

Annabeth grew silent for a long moment before she spoke. "I never thought I could run from such a place. Once you are in, you are there forever, but for the first time, I was running away and knew that he had no hold on me. I knew that I could get away. Thank you for coming back for me when my horse fell."

"Why would I do otherwise?"

Annabeth shrugged off the question.

His arms tightened around her. "I would never do anything else."

She blushed uncomfortably, and their ride continued in silence.

As the sun was setting, they approached the crossroads where they were supposed to meet. The sound of familiar voices met their ears. All were well and waiting.

"Anna!" squealed Christina.

In a moment, Annabeth had slipped from underneath Ransom's arm and onto the ground, where she met Christina's headlong embrace.

"Don't the pair of you make a funny looking lot," laughed the prince.

Annabeth laughed and Christina tried not to look offended.

"You'd look funny in a dress, if you had to wear one," retorted Christina, holding her chin up high.

Annabeth looked at the prince's strong six-foot figure and held back a laugh.

The prince, however, came to his own defense. "They'd have to find one to fit me first, and I don't think it would be a bit flattering."

They all laughed except Christina; Ransom kindly changed the subject.

"Well, standing here talking will only get us caught, so I suggest we move on."

Both girls looked gratefully at him and Annabeth came back to his side to mount again.

"Where is your horse, Annabeth?" asked Song Lark.

"He went down two days ago in a hare's hole when we were running, and Ransom came back for me," she answered softly.

"Your horse must be weary from carrying both of you. Anna, why don't you ride behind me? I'd take Christina but she is mad at me. Aren't you, Christina?" asked Alf.

Christina didn't deem it necessary to reply.

"Song Lark, will you be so kind to help me up?" she asked, turning to him, her mouth held in a prim manner.

Song Lark laughed and offered her his hand, sliding his foot from his stirrup.

Annabeth looked up at Ransom, asking for his opinion. He nodded her forward and a moment later Alf was by her side offering her his hand. Taking it, she leapt up behind him. The prince took the lead with Song Lark following, leaving Ransom to bring up the rear.

As the sky grew darker, the stars came out, and the moon rose, Song Lark ran his fingers over his lute, humming a few lines of a new refrain he was making up in his mind.

Ransom watched as the music slowly relaxed Christina. Her head came to rest on Song Lark's shoulder, her body became limp, her breathing rhythmic and deep as she fell asleep. His eyes passed Song Lark to Prince Alfred and Annabeth. They were silent, and Annabeth seemed more interested in the dark silhouette of passing trees than anything else. When the moon began to set in the sky, they searched for a place to make camp.

The next morning, Annabeth dragged her eyes open. That was the one thing she hated about living on the run—late nights and early mornings. Stretching, she felt the chill of the early morning gnaw at her stiff and weary body; her back ached from the hard ground. Reluctantly, she pushed herself up to a sitting position. Looking to her right, she noticed that Christina was still out to the world, her entire body limp with weariness. Song Lark was seated against a tree, his eyes still firmly shut, while Alf was building a fire.

"Alf, where is Ransom?"

"He went fishing," he answered with a nod toward the river. "Now go back to sleep."

"Can't; I am too cold."

"Come get warm by the fire, then."

Annabeth came to the fire, still wrapped in her cloak, and held her hands out over the ambitious orange and yellow flames as they began to grow.

In a little while, Christina joined them, the cold having awakened her as well. In a few minutes she had fallen asleep again—exhausted, her head resting on Annabeth's cloak.

The wood popped restlessly; the logs shifted. She looked up to see Prince Alfred looking at her across the fire.

"What?" she asked.

"Why haven't you asked me?"

"I guess I am scared of what you will say, and sometimes not knowing is..."

He nodded. "Better than knowing. It leaves you to imagine the worst and best possible, without being tied to the facts."

Annabeth nodded and looked down at the fire.

"I've seen him; he's holding his own, Annabeth." Prince Alfred came to her side and wrapped his arm around her shoulder. "He is holding his own very bravely, despite Lord Raburn and his torture," he said in a quiet voice.

Annabeth bit her lower lip hard.

"You knew that would happen, didn't you?"

She nodded. "It's just so difficult to hear it…" She sighed.

"Actually said?"

She nodded.

"But you know Raburn. He does everything in style and likes even his enemies to live as long as possible. He has been treated well, if you can call living in a dungeon that. But he hasn't laid his hand against him for the last two months. Your father wouldn't budge, and he knows it is useless to try and make him. I told him about everything you are doing out here, and he is proud of you, Annabeth. Prouder than a peacock. His daughter is thwarting one of the most powerful men this country has ever known, and every day that you are free is a day he lives free in his soul."

"Oh, Alf." Annabeth laid her head against his shoulder.

"It's going to come out right in the end, Anna. Everything will come right; don't cry now," he said, pressing a brotherly kiss to her temple.

"Thank you, Alf."

"Thank you, Anna. I wouldn't be here if it weren't for you."

Annabeth only smiled and sighed, resting her

chin against her closely drawn knee. Alf reached for another stick to lay on the fire and glanced over his shoulder.

"Hello, Ransom. You are back soon."

"Fishing was good," he said, holding up the catch he had already cleaned.

In a few minutes the three of them were roasting fish over the fire.

When the food was ready, they awoke Lady Christina and Song Lark, and they all feasted.

"You certainly know how to roast good fish," commented Song Lark to Ransom as his last piece disappeared.

"By the way, Song Lark, where are the rest of the supplies that were supposed to be in your saddlebags? I couldn't find them this morning," said Ransom.

"Oh, that," pulled out Song Lark with a long breath.

Prince Alf's face twisted with a mixed expression of amusement and pain. "I am afraid that we were all rather hungry on our first night out of prison."

"Is that so. Well, that means we won't be able to eat until we reach the border, for Annabeth and I only had dried food and that is all gone, too," said Ransom with a long sigh, glancing accusingly around the group.

"I woke up in the middle of the night and was hungry. Since these two ate me out of house and home, I had to raid your saddlebags," protested Song Lark in his defense.

"I don't know why you keep dragging me into your trouble," said Christina, a pout pulling at her lips.

"What is wrong with her, Annabeth? She hasn't said a civil word to me all day," said Prince Alfred teasingly.

At this, Christina burst into tears and, rising to her feet, ran to the edge of camp, not daring to go a step further.

Annabeth shook her head at him. "Did you need to be *so* insensitive? She isn't used to this lifestyle. She has never had a day of rough riding or living in her life. Christina is exhausted and she needs your kindness and not your criticism, even if it is in fun."

Annabeth sighed and put down her fish, getting ready to stand up and go talk to Christina, when Alf's hand stayed her.

"I'll go talk to her. I am the one who caused the problem."

Annabeth watched as he approached her. His shoulders hunched to Christina's level, he stood just a little behind, whispering in her ear.

In a minute she had turned and was crying into his shirt; in a few minutes more they were sitting on a log talking.

Annabeth turned around.

"Where is Song Lark?"

"He went for supplies; he says the two of them could talk all morning, and I am pretty sure that we have lost Raburn. We all need a rest; we've been driving hard, and if we keep up a pace like we have been the horses will go lame. We'll take the morning easy and be to the border well before sundown."

"Are you sure?"

"I am sure of it."

Letting out a long sigh, she glanced over her shoulder. They were still talking in earnest, the tears had ceased to flow, and Christina was now beaming smiles and laughs.

Quietly, they both worked around their camp until Ransom noticed Annabeth slipping off into the woods.

He watched her go; then, glancing at Christina and Alf, who were still talking, he decided to follow her.

She was leaning against a tree, looking up into the

pale, blue sky of late summer between an interweaving of green leaves. The sun danced on them as the wind gently ruffled the uppermost leaves.

He took the tree across from her. Bending his knee, he leaned one foot against the trunk and folded his arms across his chest. For a long time there was silence; then Annabeth spoke.

"It's so quiet out here. I long for peace like this."

"Unlike the two birds back at camp."

"I think they could talk forever, and that is a good thing."

"Are you jealous?" asked Ransom softly.

"Jealous? Why would I be jealous?"

"I saw you and Prince Alfred this morning."

Annabeth's brow wrinkled in confusion. "I don't think I know what you mean."

Ransom leaned over and kissed Annabeth on the temple.

Blushing, she looked down, afraid to meet his eyes. "Oh, that. That was nothing. Alf is a very good friend, but he is no more than a brother to me. A few years ago, when I was ten and he was twelve, people teased that we were sweet on each other. One day, while we were sitting by the river...

"He asked me if I wanted to marry him, and I said

no, and he answered, 'Good, 'cause I don't want to marry you, either.' So we took a vow then and there that no matter what happened, we wouldn't marry one another. Then he said, because we vowed, it was now impossible, because if a young man swore something it couldn't be retracted; but if a young lady swore something it could be retracted by her father or brother—but since we had both sworn it, it was now entirely impossible. But just in case, he took my thumb and cut it, and then cut his own, and put them together, making us blood siblings. I still have the scar." She turned over her right thumb and Ransom saw the hairline scar across it.

Ransom took her small hand in his and examined it.

Suddenly, Alf was coming towards them and Ransom gently let go of her hand.

"Was Anna here just telling you about our vow?" he asked, coming up, leaning his shoulder against Annabeth's tree.

"She was," said Ransom, leaning back against the tree, his arms folded across his chest.

"Just because I have taken a vow not to love her doesn't mean I don't dote on her," he said, curling one of her stray hairs around his fingers.

Annabeth didn't back away from him but looked confidently up into his face. "Where is Christina?"

"Song Lark brought back a dress with him from his excursion and she is putting it on, so I decided to get lost."

"Very wise of you. I wonder if she needs help."

"Probably does," Alf said, pulling her hair slightly.

"Then I better go."

Ransom watched Annabeth leave, then suddenly felt the prince's eyes on him. He had pushed away from the tree, his stance was wide, and his eyes were serious and studious, his mouth screwing slightly to the side.

"What do you want with my sister?"

"What?"

"What are your intentions towards Annabeth?"

"Why should it concern you?"

"She is practically my sister. She has no one else to look after her."

"I have been doing a pretty good job of that."

Alfred tilted his head to one side and examined Ransom, his eyes seeking to pierce anything he didn't like. "You have, but if you hurt her, you will have to answer to me."

Ransom smiled. "The same goes for you." His foot pushed away from the tree and he stepped forward;

they stood shoulder to shoulder. Turning, their eyes met, measuring each other, man to man. Ransom walked towards camp, leaving the prince to think. He arrived back at camp just as the girls appeared from the thick forest, both newly clad in dresses.

"Thank you, Lark. I haven't had a new dress in ages," said Annabeth, impulsively throwing her arms around Song Lark's neck.

"My pleasure, my dear. Now, let's see how you look," he said, holding her at arm's length. Annabeth twirled, and suddenly Ransom remembered their first fight. It was the same whirl, the whirl of a girl in a pretty new dress.

Annabeth stopped in front of him with a smile and looked up into his face.

"Do you like it?" she asked, almost too pleased with it herself to really care what he thought.

Ransom put his best foot forward and made her a sweeping bow. "You look beautiful. May I have this dance?"

Annabeth blushed at the praise, covering her face with her hands shyly.

Song Lark strummed the strings of his lute with

fervor.

"Lark, you aren't indulging him!"

To that, he only laughed, and suddenly Annabeth found her hands in Ransom's and he was whirling her around, faster and faster until the world around her was a muted blur except for Ransom's face.

When at last he stopped, neither could walk a straight step and Annabeth dropped to the ground, holding her sides as she laughed. Ransom sat up and looked at her; she had laughed so hard tears had come into her eyes. Sitting up, she wiped them away.

"Well, if we are ever going to elude that horrible Raburn, I suppose we better get a move on," she sighed, rising on wobbling feet.

In a matter of minutes, they were mounting and Prince Alfred had taken up Christina behind himself, Song Lark the supplies, and Ransom, Annabeth.

CHAPTER 14

It was early afternoon when they reached a river and stopped to water their horses.

Ransom sighed with satisfaction. "We've made good time. Cross this river and go through that wood, and we'll be in my country."

"Do you really think King Harold will help us?" asked Alf, an edge of unease in his voice.

"I know he will. Your grandmother was his aunt; your father and he are cousins. I don't see how he could well refuse."

Annabeth and Prince Alfred were given the responsibility of filling the water canteens. Christina was left to stretch, while Song Lark and Ransom were in charge of watering the horses.

"I can't believe this is almost over," murmured Prince Alfred.

Annabeth didn't answer, but watched her canteen slowly fill. Unexpectedly, there was a splash of water on her cheek.

She looked at Prince Alfred indignantly; his fingertips were wet. "What was that for?"

"Not listening to your prince."

"Really?"

He smiled and went back to filling his canteen.

Annabeth bit back a smile as she cupped her hand into the water and bent as if to drink. At the last moment, she splashed it at the prince.

"Hey!" Dropping his canteen, he pulled out his sword.

Annabeth squealed and ran along the bank, Song Lark having her sword for his own lack of one, leaving her defenseless. A moment later, Prince Alfred was hot on her heels. "Save me, Ransom!" she screamed girlishly, whirling behind him and clutching his doublet as a shield.

"Aw, come, you aren't playing fair, Anna," Alf said, sliding to a halt.

Her eyes peered out from behind Ransom's back. "Neither are you! How dare you attack a lady when she isn't armed?!"

"Attacking a defenseless maiden, are you? Well! On guard!" Ransom withdrew his sword, engaging Prince Alfred in a playful battle. A moment later, Alfred's sword went flying through the air and into Ransom's hand.

"Now, let that be a lesson to you."

"How did you do that?" asked Prince Alfred,

shocked at the quickness of his demise.

Ransom only smiled, then glanced at Annabeth. She had become rigid, her eyes searching the forest.

"What is it?"

Annabeth shook her head and held up a finger requesting silence.

"I thought I heard something," she answered in a whisper after a moment.

"And I thought I saw someone in those bushes," Christina said softly.

Withdrawing her sword from Song Lark's belt, Annabeth followed the two men as they approached the bushes.

"Someone was here," said Ransom, looking at the ground; there were signs of large boot prints.

"How could I be so careless!" Annabeth scolded herself aloud.

"You weren't careless. We were all here. We should have been more diligent," said Ransom, touching her shoulder.

Annabeth shrugged it off. "We should split up. We don't have time to chase him, and there is no knowing if he is a lone spy or part of a company."

"Annabeth, help is just across the border."

"How long?" she fired.

"Before sunset at the latest."

"I am not ready to leave. Not without my father. I just can't do it, Ransom. I can't leave here."

"Anna, you of all people should leave; there is a price on your head," said Prince Alfred.

"But if he is with a force and they come after us on fresh horses, what chance do we stand? If we split up, they too will have to divide their forces. Christina needs to be somewhere safe; we can't risk her in hand-to-hand combat. Going different ways will buy us all more time."

"Annabeth, there is strength in numbers."

"Divide and conquer. I am not ready to leave. My father is here, and while there is hope of him I can't just leave." Ransom let out a sigh of disgust. "I won't leave you here to defend yourself."

"Give me until this evening. When night falls, Song Lark and I will cross the border."

"How did I get pulled into this mess?" Song Lark asked, breaking into the conversation.

"You have a horse, right? I think we need one as a distraction, unless you want to walk."

"You are right. You'll ride with me," Song Lark said with a nod.

"Then it is all decided."

Ransom and Alf glanced at each other.

"You decided, not us," replied Ransom firmly.

"If you want to take me across that river, you are going to have to tie me up," she said, backing away slightly, her hand tightening on the hilt of her sword.

Ransom's orders flashed through his mind. *"Even if you have to drag her here tied."*

"I am half tempted to do just that," Ransom took a step closer.

Alf's hand arrested any further movement by Ransom. "She is right. We should divide up. If we split, it will confuse them, and the more confusion we can cause the better. Let them ride upstream about an hour or more, and then cross to join us."

"One hour, but no more," Ransom agreed, looking down at Annabeth, making sure she understood.

"One hour."

In minutes they remounted, Ransom taking Christina up before him so that, should there be an attack from behind, she would not be a shield to his back. Both parties entered the water. Ransom and the Prince headed downstream while Annabeth and Song

Lark headed up with the sword hanging once again at Annabeth's side.

"Lark, did you hear that?"

"Hear what?"

"That bird call."

Lark pulled the horse to a halt in the stream.

"I don't hear anything."

"We need to cross now and make a run for it. They've found us."

"How is that possible?"

"I don't know. It just is."

There was shrill whistle in the air, and Song Lark lurched in pain as an arrow sunk into his left shoulder, nearly grazing Annabeth' neck.

Annabeth took the reins from his hands and kicked the horse into a gallop to the other side of the stream.

"Annabeth, let me down. Take the horse and run for your life."

"No; I am not about to lose you. We've come too far for that."

Annabeth never could figure how he had done it, but in a minute he had freed himself and fell to the ground. Annabeth pulled the horse to a halt and returned.

"I am not leaving you!"

"Yes, you are. I know how to hide. Now, run for your life!"

Annabeth hesitated. He was too determined to be swayed, and staying would take away both of their chances of getting away.

Turning, she dug her heels into the horse's side, leaning forward so her head and the neck of the horse were on the same level. Shouts rose up from behind her, shouts of familiar angry voices that chilled her soul.

Without warning, she came to a wall of men on horses, swords drawn, all wearing the uniform of Lord Raburn. It was a line of thirty men.

Annabeth pulled the horse to a stop, horror surging over her. There was no way to conquer. Turning back would only put her in another hornets' nest. Annabeth turned south—it seemed the only scarce possibility that she might escape.

The line surged forward and blocked the way; she pulled out her sword and charged. It was her last hope.

In moments, they surrounded and disarmed her, pulling her to the ground. Three men kept her from moving.

A pair of polished black boots swaggered up to where she was pinned. "So this is the little girl who has been causing all of the trouble."

She didn't reply.

"On her feet."

They jerked her up, and Annabeth looked up at a man she had never seen in Lord Raburn's service. His face was cold and hardened; his dark hair fell slightly over his brow; his green eyes seemed to look into her soul.

"Tell me, is your name Annabeth?"

For a moment, for the mere amusement of trying to annoy him, she thought to pretend innocence by lying and saying her name was Rose and she was a mere dairymaid. Instead, she remained silent.

"Are you going to answer my question?"

"Would you believe me if I told you otherwise?" she finally answered.

"No, I don't think I would. After all, you answer perfectly to this description," and he pulled out a scroll of paper and read it aloud. "You seem to answer to it perfectly, don't you agree?"

"It all depends on how you look at it."

A heavy blow resounded on her cheekbone, making her dizzy, and she would have fallen to the ground if they hadn't had such a deathly grip on her arms.

"Can't you answer him respectfully?" spat out the man who had delivered his fist to her jaw.

For a moment, she couldn't answer. Everything seemed a blur around her. She saw the hand raised again and turned away, closing her eyes.

"Honestly, there is no need to be so harsh on the girl."

"She has kept us on the…"

"I know, but we have her now and there is no need for brutality. I am sure she can wait for the torture chamber."

At those words, Annabeth's heart gave a cold shudder in her chest.

"But if we do it now, it could be even worse for her there."

"He said he wanted her delivered unharmed. If you can't restrain your passion against a mere girl, I shall have to do something serious about it. Now, where is the prince?"

"What prince?"

"The one you helped escape."

"It's nothing but a rumor. A rumor told to make us all believe the prince is alive when he is really dead. Isn't it?" Her jaw tightened; she couldn't give them ground to torture her on; she needed to give the others time to escape.

"You would doubt my word?"

"I have no idea who you are and no desire to respect a servant of my enemy."

"Are you trying to insult me?"

"I did insult you. You are just too thick to realize it."

He caught her chin and looked piercingly into her eyes. His fingers tightened around her already swelling jaw. She winced at the unexpected pain.

"Don't you dare speak to me like that again."

"I don't even know who you are."

"I replaced your father. I am Eliot Rath, the new captain of the guard, and once Lord Raburn is king, I will be one of the most powerful men in the land. Don't toy with me, or you will find yourself in a very, very sorry position. Understood?"

Something about his coldness chilled her. It was calculated and seemingly heartless. Shivers snaked up her spine.

Taking chains from his saddlebag, he came to her, his mouth twisted in a smile.

Her heart sank as a cold feeling turned in her stomach.

"Never thought you'd see these, did you?"

He clamped the neck ring with a cold click around her throat.

Annabeth moved to strike him with a kick; she wouldn't go down without a fight. She found her leg caught and spun, landing painfully face-first on the ground. His knee sank into her back, expelling the air from her lungs.

In a moment all her air was gone, and she couldn't breathe in. His mouth hovered by her ear.

"You should have let Ransom capture you," he whispered.

What did he just say? Ransom? Capture? How does he know Ransom?

The question made her thoughts feel fuzzy. She tried to breath in; it wouldn't come. Dark dots danced in front of her eyes; everything started turning black.

He jerked Annabeth to her feet, clamping chains on her wrists, but she was too dizzy to even think of resisting. He mounted and pulled Annabeth into the saddle in front of him, jailing her between his arms.

"Shouldn't we have her ride alone, Captain?"

"I am not risking her getting any ideas. This way I'll know exactly what she is up to."

They spurred their horses into a gallop and headed towards Anondorf Castle.

CHAPTER 15

With great care, the three forged their way downstream and onto the opposite bank. They galloped across an open field and entered a tall dark wood.

Christina shivered against Ransom, and suddenly half a dozen men with drawn bows were around them.

"Halt! Who goes there?"

"Brankin!" shouted Ransom in recognition.

"Ransom, is that you?"

The man moved closer. "Why I'll be, it *is* you. Is that Annabeth?" he asked, nodding towards Christina.

"No, Brankin. I would like you to meet Prince Alfred and Lady Christina."

"So, you couldn't find her? Eh. She was too elusive even for the great soldier, bounty hunter, tracker, Ransom."

"No, I found her. She'll be here later with the famous minstrel, Song Lark."

"You are a bounty hunter?" asked Alf, suddenly ill at ease.

"Among other things," answered Ransom calmly, with a smile.

"Well, come on, you are wasting time and your father will be delighted to see you, Prince Alfred," said Brankin

"What? *My* father?" asked the Prince, baffled.

"Yes, your father. When he found out there was trouble here he came back in disguise and asked King Harold for his help. His men just finished fighting a war, and he doesn't want to send them into another without aid."

Coming through the forest, they arrived at a bustling camp filled with a ready army. Swords were being sharpened, arrows fitted with feathers and notched into bows, and armor polished to shining perfection. They came to the largest tent surrounded by guards. Dismounting, all were given immediate entrance.

Ransom watched as the father and son reunited. A lump rising in his throat, he glanced at his king who motioned him into the adjoining tent.

"You have anticipated my next request, but failed my first."

"Annabeth will be here by tonight, your majesty. We were being followed and decided to split up."

"Well, that is good, because we need her."

Ransom's brow wrinkled. "What? I am sorry,

sire?"

"We need to know everything she knows about Anondorf, and then we will have to turn her over to Eliot."

"I don't understand, your majesty."

"Eliot has managed to make himself Raburn's new captain of the guard. Unfortunately, he has not been able to pass along any information, all of our scouts have never returned, and I am unwilling to send in my forces without knowing the layout. From what I have heard, the place is a death trap."

"You aren't thinking of letting him turn her in."

"I don't see that I have much of a choice. One of our would meet him in the handoff, then we could the information we need and Eliot can set them up for failure within the castle. We have failed in extracting any information from Raburn's men; they are terrified of the man, and would rather die with his secrets than reveal them. I am not about to send my men into the lion's jaws without the layout of the place."

"Sire, I was there. I can tell you what it was like. Song Lark was there; he will tell you, and Annabeth—she knows every corner of the place. You don't need to turn her in to get the information. Eliot doesn't have to do anything, just get out."

"You really think that you can tell us everything we need to know?"

"A good deal of it."

"Start mapping it out," he said, pushing quill and parchment towards Ransom. "I'll see what kind of a message I can get to Eliot. His spy should be reporting back any time now to let me know what is going on."

Nearly an hour later, Ransom pushed away the parchment and quill. It was in the deepest detail he could remember. Wearing the monk's hood hadn't helped him much; hopefully Song Lark and Annabeth would know more.

Restlessness swept over Ransom. Something was wrong, desperately wrong. He looked at the sky. It was as blue and perfect as any heart could wish.

Pacing in front of the tent, he stamped his foot impatiently. They should arrive there at any time.

Readying a fresh horse, he decided to search for them.

"Hello, Ransom," offered a voice near at hand as he tightened the saddle strap. "Where are you off to?"

"Just around."

"Well, you don't have to bother looking for Annabeth anymore."

"What?"

The man smiled. "Eliot has her. Do you know where the king is?"

Numbness paralyzed Ransom's heart, but he kept moving like nothing had happened, just like he had trained himself. "He was in his tent just a little while ago," his voice said evenly.

"Thank you! We'll have to catch up later, aye?"

He nodded and mounted. "I'll see you around."

Turning his horse's head, he turned back from where the messenger had come. Ransom dug his heels into the horse's sides, spurring him into a gallop. There was no time to lose. His heart was aching, aching unbearably for Annabeth.

Arriving at the river, he stormed up the bank, hoping he would somehow find or catch them in time to stop what was going to happen next. He found the trail, then galloped out of the riverbank and followed it.

"Ransom, is that you?" asked a husky voice.

"Song Lark?" he asked, his heart flashing up in his throat.

In a moment he had located the wounded man.

"What happened to you? Where is Annabeth?"

"They've got her," he whispered hoarsely. "They couldn't find me—not that they looked, they were too happy to have her. You've got to get help. Thirty of them took her—at least."

"Thirty?" Ransom winced.

"You've got no chance against them. You have to get help."

All this while, Ransom had been tending to Song Lark's wounded shoulder; he had extracted the arrow head and was binding the wound with Song Lark's shirt.

"We'll see about that," he muttered under his breath. "Drink this. Now, how strong do you feel? Can you ride?"

"Yes."

"Good, 'cause I am going to need your help."

In a few minutes they had mounted double in on the horse. Ransom followed the trail and read the small battle scene for himself.

"She didn't stand a chance. Why didn't I just follow orders?" he muttered under his breath. Turning his horse, they galloped towards Anondorf.

CHAPTER 16

Captain Eliot and his company rode like the wind, blazing a clear, straight-as-an-arrow path towards Anondorf Castle.

It was in the light of the moon that they stopped on the crest of a hill, to view the cold monstrosity. They pulled up and looked at it in all of its glory.

"Welcome home," laughed one of the men, his voice coarse and harsh.

Annabeth's jaw tightened. All afternoon she had been praying; for what she didn't know, but something—anything different than what was happening to her now.

Unexpectedly, the new captain of the guard was whispering in her ear.

Turning away, she ignored him.

He grabbed her arm, pressuring her to listen.

"Fight me," he repeated his barely whispered words.

For a moment she froze, wondering what he could possibly mean by that. Was this the deliverance she had been praying for or a trap?

He leaned away from her, letting his laugh cackle. It sounded evil in the moonlight. Anger surged through her veins. Moving her elbow to one side, she used it as a weapon, jabbing him in the ribs. He started to buckle. She turned, digging her elbow high into his chest. He seemed to bend half over in the saddle, trying to catch his breath.

Annabeth moved to try and take control, but one of his arms arrested her movements. His other hand was holding a cloth over her mouth and nose, bending her head back against his shoulder.

She tried to fight it, but he had her immobile and surprised.

"Sorry, but it is the only way I could think to make it easy on you," he seemed to whisper in her ear as a fog whirled around her brain. Annabeth wished he would stop whispering in her ear; it was confusing. Who was he really, and why...?

She never got to finish that question, as unconsciousness, gray, dark, and unknown, spiraled around her like a dream.

The dark feeling was leaving her. Her head ached; a dizzy feeling went round and round in her brain.

The cold stone stole away Annabeth's core heat. The chill seeped towards her bones like icy needles. But it wasn't the chill that made her heart freeze in horror, wanting the gray to take her back into its restless folds. It was the dark, cold presence of Lord Raburn.

She could feel him before she regained consciousness; it was a suffocating feeling that pressed the life out of her.

Hesitant, she opened her eyes, her body aching from the cold. There was no light, save for the moon, who showed his innocent round face through the windows.

Annabeth pushed herself slowly upright with her bound hands, sitting in a pool of moonlight. She did not rise to her feet; he was there hiding in the darkness. Turning slightly to her right, she saw his outline in the shadows. Bowing her head, Annabeth waited, trying to make the dizzy feeling pass away. She needed all of her wits about her. She had seen enough of his torture sessions in the great hall and dungeon to know how they went.

Slowly.

Deliberately, he walked toward her. His steps echoed in the room until he was standing before her.

"Hello, Annabeth."

The words ran a chill down her spine. She didn't move.

"Aren't you going to greet the man who has been a second father to you? You've been gone far too long. I've missed you."

Annabeth still did not move.

He took a step to the side, blocking the moonlight from reaching her.

"I am disappointed in you, Annabeth. You want to know why?"

Mentally, Annabeth registered that answer as a no, but refused to answer out loud. She would need to save her strength for the real battle.

"Do you care at all, Annabeth, that you have disappointed me?"

Her desire to fight back got the best of her. "What is there to disappoint?"

For a long minute, there was complete silence. The chilling silence let Annabeth reprimand her quick tongue with a vengeance.

"I'll forget I heard that, under the pretense that spending so much time in the wilderness has made you forget the manners that I have struggled to teach you."

He stepped away, his step echoing in the bare hall. He was standing behind her. Annabeth waited for the crushing blow that would send her flying face first to the stone. She had seen him do it often enough. There were reasons she hadn't gotten to her feet.

He laid his hand softly on her shoulder. If he had been a kind person, the touch would have been tender, but she knew he was just waiting.

"You know why I am disappointed in you, Annabeth?" The grip tightened on her shoulder.

Annabeth didn't answer. He would answer his own question. Eventually.

The grip loosened. Now she lay in the greatest danger of all and she must answer his questions carefully, but above all, she must answer.

"You betrayed me. Do you have any idea what it feels like to be betrayed?"

"I might, since you have been doing it to me since I was a child."

He laughed. "So you remember, do you?"

"You always got my secrets from me and then betrayed me in front of the entire hall. You taught me not to trust you."

"Those are mere childish offenses; nothing more. I was only trying to get to your father. Nothing spurs a man to prove himself to you than one who has something to prove. It was a good tactic. But I don't understand why you betrayed me to your father after all that I did for you."

"I don't owe you anything, and he deserved the truth," Annabeth held her tongue from lashing out in further anger.

A moment later, she was flat on her back with the feeling of stone echoing through her head. Opening her blurry eyes, she saw him sheath the dagger in his boot. At least she had saved herself that pain.

He leaned his whole body's weight on one of her shoulders. "Annabeth, you know, now that I have you, your life is useless to me."

She closed her eyes, trying to make her head stop aching so she could comprehend what he was saying.

A moment later, the prick of a dagger made everything clear. She nodded, opening her eyes. It was sheathed again.

"What are you waiting for?" she answered.

"I have your father in the dungeon. I broke him, and he told me everything you told him by the riverbank. Like a girl, you told him everything."

"I am a girl," she answered through gritted teeth.

He snorted through his nose.

"You are right; I had almost forgotten you are a girl. A gullible little girl who always wanted to believe the best in people."

His words stung her like the venom they were. She wanted to fight him; instead she let her fingernails dig into her palms. She was helpless.

"You, Annabeth, aren't worth a thing."

"What are you waiting for?" she muttered, wishing her hands were free—that *she* was free.

"Where is the prince?" his voice hissed in a sneer.

Annabeth swallowed, her heart fading for a moment within her. *Does that alone make my life valuable?*

She looked him straight in the eye. She would not give him the satisfaction of knowing she knew he was alive.

"Dead in your tower, I thought," she answered.

"You never were a good liar, Annabeth," he said softly. "Eliot. Take her downstairs and get her ready for the rack."

"Yes, my lord," said the man, stepping forward. "But it is late and you have not rested."

Raburn's temper burst into flames. "And I will not rest until the prince is found!"

"Yes, my lord."

Raburn's voice gentled again. "Take her to the rack, and make sure her father is present. I want him bound and gagged."

Annabeth mentally winced. To see her father, and like this, after so many months…but this was a capture she could not have avoided. Unless she had gone with Ransom.

Oh, Ransom, where are you?

She didn't have long to linger over the question as Eliot pulled her to her feet and started pulling her towards the dungeon. Suddenly, her body was shivering with cold. It felt as if the stone floor had melted into her.

"Are you afraid?" asked Eliot, turning to her.

"No," she answered through chattering teeth. "Just cold."

His hand touched hers. He felt like a flame against her ice-cold fingers.

With every step she took, something inside of her wanted to scream. To fight. To not move an inch. To make a scene for the first time in her life. To make Captain Eliot drag her kicking and screaming into the hell of Raburn's making.

Instead, she walked, breathing slow, calm gasps of air. For months she had seen this as the dreadful ending; she had known it would come, and now it had. She would not give Raburn the gratification of her fear.

She could not lose control of herself.

She must not.

Tears sprang into her eyes. She blinked them back fiercely. People who lost it before they stepped into the dungeon broke at the slightest provocation. People who did not lasted.

Annabeth set her jaw with determination. She would last. She would prevail. She would not give up. For the sake of the crown, for Prince Alfred's future, she mustn't give an inch.

She must last.

Her heart quivered in her chest; she screwed her mouth tightly and blinked back the threatening tears. In that blink, a face flashed before her eyes, and it wasn't that of his highness.

There was no hope. Her cause was dead, but he—he would keep her cause safe.

At the top of the stairs they halted, and Annabeth gathered herself. This was it. Fighting this hollow fate would only make it worse; she numbed her mind to the horror of it. She mustn't think about it. She moved her mind into a place of existence. Annabeth shoved aside the rancid smell of decay, the bleak stone walls dripping with water, the sputtering torches; they all became a mere blur.

Suddenly, though, *it* was in front of her. Images flashed through her mind. She had seen victims tortured, and they had kept her in silence until now. Their memories had bound her mouth tightly with secrets.

But now it was waiting for her. She stopped in her tracks. Taking one gasp of horror, she looked up at Eliot. Something in her wanted to break down—to plead for her life as she had seen so many others do. His eyes were cold and prepared.

A few moments later, she heard a shuffling in the hall. In a familiar presence warmed the room: a presence that she loved dearly and had been often deprived of. She felt her heart crack in her chest.

Annabeth waited until she knew she could keep back the tears before she raised her eyes to meet her father's. They were grieved, pale, blue eyes that looked into hers, but there was a touch of compassion and love in them. She knew that he loved her, though no words passed between them.

Having him see her pain and humiliation was torture all its own.

In too short a time, Raburn came down, a gloating smile on his face.

"Well, well. I am glad to see we are all back

together again. Now you can make this a truly happy reunion, and just tell me where Prince Alfred is. Because if you do that, I will set you free from your bonds and your father's and make a poor mere peasant girl some sort of pretty little duchess in my kingdom. What do you say?" he asked, stroking her cheek in an affectionate manner.

"You would do nothing of the sort," Annabeth replied flatly. She knew too well how he made and broke his promises.

Somehow he smiled as he gave the order. "Put her on the rack."

Four men stepped forward at his command. Eliot unlocked her bonds, and Annabeth found herself pinned to the long table with each man holding down one of her limbs.

"You know how this goes, Annabeth. I ask you four questions, and your answers decide whether you get tied to the rack or are set free. Now, the question is very simple. Where is the prince, Annabeth?"

"You already asked me that."

"But I did not receive a proper answer."

There was a long pause. Raburn nodded. The rope was tied securely to her right hand.

"Where is the prince, Annabeth?"

She buttoned her mouth shut, tightening her jaw with resolution.

A rope was firmly attached to her left leg.

"Annabeth, I am not sure how you got into my castle, but I know you did. You helped the prince leave my care and protection. Now, where is he?"

"I don't know."

It was now her left hand that lost its freedom to the rack.

"Annabeth, where is Christina?"

She looked up at the ceiling. That was her final answer.

She phased out the sound of his voice talking and the rack tightened one notch, pulling the ropes tight.

Annabeth stared at the stones above her. She would not let Lord Raburn get to her; he would not break her.

Pain increased as her body stretched, but it was no worse than she had expected. One notch at a time it grew worse, and his voice became harder to obscure in her head. She let her thoughts weave panicked trails through her mind, trying to escape the bitter reality of the device that gripped her.

Without warning, the ropes jerked her body as the wheel turned three notches in one smooth roll.

Annabeth couldn't help the scream. Something on the right side of her body gave way and there was a shuddering pop in her shoulder.

A moment later the ropes slackened, and she was released. Her body sagged. She could not try to move as the pain seemed to seep into every bone in her body.

There was dampness on her right side. Her wound, so newly healed, had given way beneath the jerk, and now blood was soaking her dress.

Annabeth was wrenched from the rack and pushed to her knees before Lord Raburn. He touched her shoulder.

"Hold still now." With a sudden and calculating yank, the shoulder jolted back into place. Annabeth screamed, falling forward, blackness reaching to catch her in its arms of mercy.

CHAPTER 17

Annabeth knew from the feeling of the room that Captain Eliot was standing before her, hands resting on his hips, his stance wide, and his shoulders squared. He was staring at her—it felt more like he was staring *through* her. It was his hands that had twisted the wheel of the rack.

Numbly, she wondered how she was standing. What was holding her up?

Captain Eliot seemed to sense her coming to consciousness. Moving forward, he tilted her head back and poured water between her parched lips. The movement of her head rippled a spasm of pain through her body, and she sagged against the cold damp wall, realizing what was holding her up despite her weakness.

Chains with weights pulled at her arms, held her upright even as her legs were unsteady as water beneath her. The weights held her, forcing her against the cold wall. Her mind sought for refuge, but torment haunted every corner of her existence—numb, blaring, searing, and pulsating through her core. Her head seemed to swim in circles; Annabeth knew there would be no stopping it.

Eliot was silent. His hands barely touched her wound. Pain seized her and she let out a cry as a chill ran through her body. Waves of hot and cold pulled her into a whirlpool of agony.

The gentleness in his touch was strange as he bound her wound, but even his lightest touch of mercy caused anguish to gnaw through her worse than before.

Something strange pricked her heart and mind awake as he finished. She shoved it aside.

"Lord Raburn told me you'll have a day to think over your decision. If it doesn't change, you go back on the rack." His voice was steel-like, and he turned to go.

The words pricked her mind again, and she wanted to push them away. Then the thought flashed through her mind:

"*For Ransom's sake, tell him.*"

"Be careful of Raburn's wine."

"What?"

Using up her strength she repeated the words. "Be careful of Raburn's wine. It loosens the tongue more than most."

His cool hand was pressing against her hot cheek, sweeping a stray hair away from her face.

"I will be."

Then he was gone and Annabeth was left with the numbing pain in every atom of her body.

Chapter 18

Dawn rose, and Ransom sat at the edge of the woods, staring at Anondorf. Song Lark was sound asleep. He would have to wait for the right time. He couldn't seem too eager.

He was Ransom, the bounty hunter who had tracked his prey back to Anondorf Castle and wanted to see the elusive and fabled Annabeth for himself.

It was near midmorning when he decided it was time to make his appearance and request entrance at Anondorf Castle.

"Who goes there, and what do you want?" asked an unpleasant voice from the top of the castle.

"I am a bounty hunter looking for work. I heard this is the place to come."

There was a murmur at the top of the castle walls, and one of the guards disappeared.

Several minutes later, the drawbridge was lowered and the gate opened. Ransom rode through.

In the middle of the courtyard he was halted; a stable boy took his horse. Dismounting, he casually followed the guard.

He was shown into a large chamber that resembled something after the manner of a throne room in its grandeur. Eliot stood beside Lord Raburn's chair, looking slightly surprised. Ransom ignored him.

Ransom bowed low. "My lord," he said reverently.

"So I hear you are a bounty hunter."

"That I am. The best one in every country that I have been in."

Lord Raburn laughed shallowly. "Is that so?"

"I was on Annabeth's trail, and when I found out it led here, I thought I would see if it was true that she was caught."

"Really?"

"Truly, my lord. I was less than a day behind her, and catching up rather quickly. It appeared as if she was traveling in a party of three or four."

"It is true, she was. Unfortunately, according to my captain, their trail disappeared into thin air, but they did catch the worst of the culprits."

"So, it is true you have her."

"Yes, it is true."

"Would it be possible to see her?"

"I don't see why not. Eliot, bring her up here. I think she needs a break from the dungeon. Being down there too long can be hard on the soul."

The cell door creaked open. A key unlocked the chain that bound her to the wall, jerking her body to one side.

Annabeth gasped in agony as it washed cruelly over her in a fresh deep pang, causing the pain to soar through her body and pound through her brain.

"Not yet," she whispered hoarsely, the fresh pain breaking words from her that she did not wish to say. "Not the rack; not yet."

"You have a visitor. Ransom, a bounty hunter, has come to see you."

At the word *Ransom* her mind jerked away from the pain into full consciousness.

"What?" she asked, her eyes clearing from the blur of agony.

Eliot looked at her and, placing his hand on the wall, leaned close in the low flickering light of the torches, searching her eyes.

"You know him, don't you?" he whispered quietly.

"No, I don't," she said, trying to twist away. Annabeth was shocked to find herself so disabled. Her limbs felt hollow, but rippled with inexhaustible wells of suffering. Any command given to move only brought torture and a frozen feeling to her body.

"Raburn always said you were a poor liar."

"I never had the chance to lie to him," she answered, seeking for a weapon in her words, only to make a confession. Her eyes glanced wincingly up into Eliot's.

"I don't wish to see anyone." The very thought of stepping outside of her cell was exhausting.

"Come on," he said with an unexpected gentleness, pulling her arm against her body with a sling. "This way you won't hurt too badly."

Annabeth was unsure exactly how she arrived at the tall set of double doors that led into Raburn's hearing room, but she was standing there. A gray numbness gnawing at her while unconsciousness stood ready to sweep her unsteady feet out from under her and carry her away into the comfort of oblivion and darkness.

Eliot turned her and lifted her chin to look into his eyes.

"Whatever you do, do not betray him."

The words and meaning seemed blurred. Annabeth just wanted to sink into nothingness—to never be.

With a powerful stroke of his hands, he opened the doors and led her in. Annabeth kept her eyes on the floor.

"So this is the famous Annabeth," said a cold but familiar voice.

Annabeth had never known a voice to carry so much power. She wanted to cry. To have him standing there in that room, to have Ransom see her like this, was going to break her into pieces.

"Annabeth, you have a visitor. Aren't you going to greet him?"

"No," she whispered hoarsely, without raising her head.

"Eliot, make Annabeth show her manners."

Annabeth could feel him moving towards her. She wondered what cruelty he would think of. Then, Ransom was by her side.

"No need. I can do it myself. A cruel hand like yours could break a girl needlessly," he said, taking her chin and lifting it to meet his face.

Annabeth closed her eyes. She did not want to see him, yet everything within her longed for him.

Ransom laid a cool hand on her neck that burned from the tense pull of the chains. He leaned close, whispering, "Look at me."

His hand pressured her neck. The pain caused her eyes to open in wounded surprise.

Raburn laughed from behind them. "You have a way with the girl."

Ransom's hand dropped to his side; he turned slightly to face Lord Raburn. "I like girls who know their mind. I find they need a special touch," he said, brushing the back of his hand over her cheek.

Annabeth let her eyes sink wounded daggers into him. *What is he thinking?*

Ransom walked casually around Annabeth in circles, taking in every inch of her frame.

"Are you taken with her?" asked Lord Raburn, sounding rather amused from his throne-like chair.

"I must admit," he let out rather reluctantly, "I am. She is such a helpless looking little thing, I can hardly believe she eluded me."

Raburn laughed. "She is a crafty little thing."

"Yes, I am afraid so." Ransom stopped his circling and stared at Annabeth for a long time, and then he whirled around. "But she is beside the point. I came here to see if you had any other work that you could offer me. I have a good reputation in the kingdom of Falway and am ready to prove myself here."

Raburn looked at him piercingly.

Ransom lowered his eyes and looked up at him sideways, a sly charm easing from him. "I've heard rumors that the prince has been quite a disobedient problem, and stands in need of a firm correction."

"You would be correct, Ransom."

"If he is indeed the other part of the group that was riding with Annabeth, they have reached Falway. There is no better man than myself to track him down and bring him back to you unharmed."

"Unharmed, you say?"

"Yes, my lord." He let a long pause drift in the conversation. "Unless some unfortunate accident happened to take place, my lord."

"You are a keen man, Ransom."

"I could easily make it look like the prince was killed by some stray Falway noble who murdered him in cold blood. I would drag the body back here and you could lift it up as an outrageous insult to your people."

"A war might start between your country and mine."

"I couldn't care less. My loyalty is to my satisfaction and whoever serves it."

"Then consider yourself commissioned. Your pay will be excellent, I promise."

"Thank you, my lord. I shall fulfill my duty with

all diligence." Turning to leave, he stopped beside Annabeth. Reaching out, Ransom touched her chin, turning her to face him. Annabeth pulled away, wounded and betrayed.

Gently he repeated the action, more firmly; preventing her head from lurching away.

Slowly, painfully, she opened her eyes and looked at him, tears coming into them. Suddenly, Annabeth didn't care if she cried.

Where is the Ransom I know? What in the world is going on?

Unexpectedly, Lord Raburn spoke. "You know, Ransom, letting her live with the knowledge she failed would be the worst torture she could ever face."

"I've no doubt about that. She is the kind that would feel it keenly all of her days." Ransom looked into her eyes, now welling with tears. He wanted to reach out and harbor her in his arms, to make all the pain she was suffering fall away from her body.

"Then, if you want her, you may have her when you return; she will be a bonus to your reward."

Ransom nodded. "That suits me perfectly, my lord."

"It suits us both."

"Consider it done, then. I'll be back in a week to claim my prize," said Ransom, stroking her cheek.

She turned away; he let her slip past his hand.

"Annabeth," he said almost under his breath.

Unexpectedly, she turned to him. "When you return, there will be nothing of me left. I suggest you choose your next step wisely. Men who live by the sword die by the sword."

Ransom looked into her eyes, letting questions race through his, hoping she could read them. "Are you ready to meet what fate he has for you?" he nodded towards Lord Raburn.

Annabeth swallowed; she was resigned. "I have been ready for the last few months. The time has come."

"We'll see about that," he said, and he walked past her.

Suddenly, Eliot's chest collided into his, hands gripped his vest.

"Don't you ever dare overstep your bounds with me again. He gave me the order."

"Keep your hands off me," said Ransom. Grabbing Eliot's fist, he pushed it away. As he did so, he felt a piece of paper pressed into his hand.

Bristling, they passed each other, rubbing angry shoulders.

CHAPTER 19

Ransom walked swiftly into the courtyard, still bristling from his encounter with Eliot, his fists tightly clenched. Before mounting, Ransom adjusted his boots; sliding the piece of paper that Eliot had put in his hand carefully between his concealed dagger and his leg.

He would not think of Annabeth until he was outside the gate, lest it show on his face. He smiled at the stable boy and flipped him a trifling coin.

"Thanks for taking care of him for me."

Barely touching the stirrup, he leapt into the saddle and galloped through the gate. In a moment he was gone, and he let what he had seen run through him.

Annabeth. *My Annabeth.* He had never dreamed he could see her in more pain than when he had first met her. She was torn—wounded inside and out. She would not last long in that dungeon. It would not break her will, but it had already shattered her spirit; it was killing her.

He could not reach where he had hidden Song Lark soon enough. There would be no time to wait for King Harold to come with his soldiers to attack. Lord

Raburn was the kind of man who would torture her for his own amusement. He longed to sink a dagger into the man's chest—to *make* him feel all the pain he had ever caused Annabeth, her father, and his other victims.

Ransom knew he would have to storm the castle.

Alone.

"It appears, my dear Annabeth, that you have a knight in shining armor come to rescue you from my wicked dungeon. What he doesn't know is when he arrives back in a week, he will find you dead, and then I shall finish him off too in the dungeon. Best way for a rich man to save himself money: hire bounty hunters, and then kill them like they did their prey." Lord Raburn laughed as he brushed past Annabeth, upsetting her balance. She tottered, then fell to the floor. Pain jolted through her, fraying every nerve, twisting every muscle, pounding round and round in her head. Resigned, she lay on the floor, too weary to care that her bed was stone.

"What do you know of this man? Eliot, he comes from your country."

"I know of him, and he is a man of his word. He will do exactly as he says. He is an honorable thief, you might say, my lord," said Eliot, his voice quiet and steady.

Raburn sighed with satisfaction. "I do feel rather indulgent today. Maybe no rack until I feel inclined. Take her back to the dungeon and put her against the wall. It breaks them soon enough."

"Yes, my lord."

Lord Raburn's satisfied footsteps faded away in the distance.

In a moment, Annabeth felt strong hands lifting her off of the cool, hard stone. She bit her lip to hold back a gasp; pain dizzied her. Her mind sought for a clear memory. Had her life never felt dizzy, or was it always like this, tumbled, torn, and screaming agony? It felt as if a lifetime had already passed away in that cell, and now she was returning to it.

Opening her eyes, Annabeth tried to focus. She had to care about what was going on around her. She must find something beyond herself and the pain if she were to know anything but this numbness as the last day of her life approached. Walking through the sunlit hallways of Raburn's castle, she tried to feel the sun's warmth, the breeze that washed its way through the windows, but to no avail. She felt nothing but the ache and pain and agony of trying to feel something different.

When they reached the stairs, she was surprised to find herself swept up in Eliot's arms as he clattered casually down the steps, then set Annabeth on her feet. He dragged her back to her cell and chained one arm to the wall.

The weights pulled and stretched the muscles in her arms, and she closed her eyes as the pain ate her consciousness.

Eliot's hand traced over her dislocated shoulder that Raburn had set.

Annabeth collapsed. It was too much.

"What were you doing there? You could have gotten yourself killed!" Song Lark's angry voice broke him out of his reverie.

"I had to know if she was still alive."

"Is she?"

Ransom nodded. "But not for long. That dungeon is killing her."

"Not Annabeth."

"You don't know what that place does to her!" Ransom turned to Song Lark, his eyes hot with anger.

"Annabeth can survive anything."

"Annabeth is not invincible. None of us are invincible." Then he added under his breath, "*I am not invincible.*"

"Then what is your plan? Are we going to go get your king?"

Ransom shook his head.

"There isn't enough time. She won't last." Ransom fished around in his boot until he came up with a slip of paper and opened it.

"Just as I expected. Song Lark, I need you to ride to the border and take this directly to King Harold. Tell them Ransom sent you, and that should get you immediate access to the king. Now, guard it with your life."

"What is it?"

"Plans for Anondorf Castle that Eliot drew up. Battle plans. Now, go."

"What are you going to do?"

Ransom looked at him.

"Do I want to know what you are going to do?"

Ransom shook his head. "No, you don't want to know."

"Godspeed to you."

"Godspeed to you, Song Lark, and may you ride like the wind."

In a moment, Song Lark was mounted and off, galloping in the distance. Ransom turned, landing a fist into a tree. He waved his hand in pain. Pulling it back, he blew on it to soothe the burning feeling. He had broken the skin in several places, leaving his hand scratched and bleeding.

"Yes, that will do. I can't hurt myself too badly."

Two hours later, a man that few would recognize walked with a slight limp down the trail to the castle.

"Who goes there?" called out the same grumpy voice.

No wonder he is such a grump. I would be too if I was left on gate duty. "Ransom, the bounty hunter. My horse broke a leg, I was wondering…"

The drawbridge lowered and Ransom limped across. Halfway across the courtyard, Eliot intercepted him.

"What do you think you are doing back here so soon?" Eliot asked between gritted and half snarling teeth. "You have a message to deliver."

"The message will be delivered shortly by a faithful hand that is not my own. I came back for Annabeth."

"He won't let her go."

"No. But maybe you will."

Eliot's eyes almost slit shut.

"Give me all the help you can. I intend to run for it."

Eliot shook his head. "You're risking your life for *her*."

"I gave her my word."

"Don't be a fool."

"Don't get your head chopped off."

Lord Raburn's voice broke into the conversation. "Eliot, is this any way to show our trusted friend how we welcome him?"

"No, my lord. I was just trying to find out why he had returned so soon and so dreadfully empty-handed," said Eliot, sharply aiming his words at Ransom.

Ransom took no notice, but bowed graciously to Lord Raburn. "My lord. I am sorry to have returned so early, but I have a request to make of you."

"Yes, and what would that be?"

"As you can see, I am horseless. My own went down and broke his leg. Being a bounty hunter can be…"

"Speak no more; we will furnish you with a horse."

"You are too kind, sir."

"It is my pleasure."

"Would it be possible, while my horse is being saddled up, that I could see Annabeth? Visit her in the dungeon."

"Are you so eager to break her into your ways?" asked Lord Raburn with a smile.

"The sooner she gets used to the thought of me, the better."

"Yes you are quite right. Snatchel, show Ransom here the way to the dungeon. The jailor will take him to Annabeth."

Ransom followed with a seeming blind ease and slight limp, but his mind was already working frantically over every last detail. Was it really possible? Everything had to be perfect.

The keys laughed mockingly in the lock, and a moment later the door creaked open, complaining of its sudden frequent usage.

"I'll call you when I am ready. I won't be long."

At the sound of Ransom's voice, pain burst freshly in her heart. Silently, she listened to the words.

"Right," answered the jailor, as he locked the door.

She felt him coming near her, his shadow falling

over her from the one flickering torch set outside her cell. A moment later, he stood only inches away, his fingers barely daring to touch her cheek.

"Annabeth." His voice was warm and gentle, as if he had put the sun into words.

"What are you doing here?"

"I've come to rescue you," he whispered. It felt as if someone had stabbed a burning knife into her heart and left it there—burning, aching, but not taking her life, just letting her exist slowly but surely. She was in so much pain already, she couldn't help her small outcry. It came bursting to the surface.

He raised her head. "Look at me, Annabeth. What is it?" He knew her cry was not one of joy, but agonizing pain.

Annabeth turned her face away. A tear trembled down her cheek making a white streak down her dirt-tarnished face.

"Annabeth," he whispered tenderly.

"Please go," she answered him, her voice shaking. Her body was weak and her heart was shaking; the last thing she wanted was to have him witness it.

"Beth, I can't."

"Please, Ransom, I have been hurt enough. There is nothing you can do. Leave me alone to die."

"What makes you think that you will die?"

She raised her eyes to meet his, letting the last layer of inner armor fall. Ransom's heart twisted in his chest.

It was gone. Her desire to live—to fight—had vanished. She was conquered, resigned. There was no spark of life, of challenge—it was only waiting: waiting for death.

"Ransom. I've lost everything; I don't want to lose you, too. Go while you can, and for my sake keep Prince Alfred safe. Please."

He sighed. "All right. You win." Leaning close, he pressed a kiss gently to her cheek.

Annabeth let the tears fall. Ransom stepped away, calling the jailor.

As the jailor looked in, he smiled at Annabeth's tears, then the wooden door grated shut between them. The keys jangled as if they enjoyed locking people up. Then there was the fatal click of the lock.

Annabeth sagged against the wall. Pain screamed through her body. She could hardly move. Her body tingled and ached; there was nothing to bring her relief. Her limbs were useless. Utterly useless. What good would they be to her even if she did get free? She tried to clench and unclench her fists. Her left responded but her right sent a ripple of agony down her arm, up her neck, and through her spine. She couldn't help the quiet whimper.

Closing her eyes, Annabeth prayed that God would be merciful—that He would take her to be with Him and her beloved mother. She couldn't stand it here on earth. Everything she loved was being torn from her, tearing her into little pieces. She didn't want to see everything she had ever loved, cherished, and tried to protect destroyed before her very eyes.

The keys were rattling in the lock again. Annabeth didn't raise her head. What was the use? Whatever came through that door would bring her more pain. Maybe, this time, it would kill her.

The door opened and someone came over, undoing her chains. The weights dropped to the floor with a crash. She raised her head as her left arm fell limp to her side.

"Ransom?" she looked up at him, barely able to breathe.

He undid her other chain. The weight landed on the stone, pulling the chain rattling after it. Annabeth's right arm dropped to her side, sending a spasm soaring through her. She wilted, but before she could fall to the floor Ransom had her in his arms,, pulling her to lean against him.

"What are you doing?" she whispered, resting her head against his strong shoulder, fighting for her own strength and willpower to push Ransom away. She couldn't even move.

"I am getting you out of here."

"No," she whimpered in protest.

"Yes, I am."

The strength in his voice sent a shiver down her spine.

"Why did you come back?"

"I promised I wouldn't leave you."

"My father?" she murmured.

"He's next, then any other unfortunate prisoners locked within these walls."

"There aren't any. He's killed the rest." She shuddered in his arms, pain making unconsciousness pull at her vision, sinking it smaller and smaller. The world seemed to rotate within her mind and she rested her head against Ransom's shoulder.

Ransom lifted Annabeth in his arms and carried her out of the cell. Opening the door to her father's cell, he saw a surprised man meet his gaze.

"What are you doing with my daughter?"

"Getting both of you out of here. Now come along."

In minutes they had climbed up the stairs of the dungeon. Ransom stopped to catch his breath and scout out the courtyard just outside the door.

His horse stood waiting near at hand. The gate was not far away; the guards were relaxed. There would be very little time that they would be surprised, but at least they wouldn't be edgy and instantly arrow-ready.

"Sir, we are going to have to spring three to a saddle. Do you think you are ready to run?"

"I am a soldier. Soldiers are always ready."

"Good, sir. When I say go, we go."

The man nodded.

Ransom shifted Annabeth in his arms. Getting her on the saddle would be painful. It was a good thing she had already blacked out, her breathing ragged but steady.

"Ready?"

"Ready," was the firm reply.

Dear God, protect us. "Go!" Ransom charged out into the courtyard, placing Annabeth in front of the saddle before mounting himself in a flash. A moment later, he turned and helped Annabeth's father up behind him.

The first cry of alarm sounded as Ransom dug his heels into the fiery steed that was to be lent to him.

"Close the gate! Pull up the drawbridge!"

But it was too late. They were through and across. A moment later, a hail of arrows rained around their defenseless backs. A second volley of arrows grazed them with nearly lethal accuracy. By the third, they knew they were gaining a healthy distance as the arrows fell wide of their intended target.

They bolted into the forest road, the horse's load too heavy to dare weaving and leaping through the twisted woods.

"Ransom! Ransom! Halt!" yelled a powerful voice, dangerously close.

"Don't stop; it's the captain of the guard," shouted Annabeth's father in Ransom's ear.

"Only him?" asked Ransom, shouting back.

"Yes."

Ransom pulled back on the reins. In a moment, Eliot pulled up beside him.

"On my horse, sir. If we are to make it, Ransom's load must be lighter."

"What?" asked Annabeth's father.

"I serve King Harold. Now hurry; we are wasting

time."

In a moment he had mounted behind Eliot. Ransom and Eliot urged their horses to the limit.

CHAPTER 20

Night fell as they crossed the border. The danger of still being pursued relaxed, and they slackened their pace.

Ransom looked down to see if Annabeth was conscious, and for the first time in that long anxious day, her blue eyes met his. With an inward sigh of relief, a smile rose to his lips.

"How are you, my Annabeth?" he whispered, not wanting the others to hear him. For just one moment he wanted her all to himself.

Her eyes were smiling through a heavy film of pain. "I can't believe you did it," she whispered, shifting in his arms to lean against his shoulder.

"We are almost there."

Riding into camp, it felt as if all eyes were turned on them. Annabeth hid her face against Ransom's doublet. He curved his shoulder, lowering his head close to shadow and protect her face.

Eliot had taken the lead and brought them to a halt before the king's tent. Ransom watched Eliot help Annabeth's father get down from the horse, then dismount himself.

"How are you, daughter?" Annabeth's father asked, taking her hand.

"Much better, thank you father," she said, trying to squeeze his hand.

Pain jolted through her arm, but it did not hurt with the dreadful throbbing of defeat. There was hope in this agony, and not despair.

"I'll help you get her down, Ransom," said Eliot, coming to their side.

Ransom shook his head. He wasn't moving for kings or countries—not if it was going to cause her pain. "I'll wait till we know where she is supposed to be."

Just then, King Harold, with Prince Alf, came from the tent.

"Well, well, what have we here?" said King Harold, breaking the silence with a serious expression.

"I always keep my word, sir," answered Ransom with a nod of his head.

"Yes, I know, but this…this outdoes them all." He turned to Eliot and for the first time saw Annabeth's father standing in his shadow.

"Garth, is that you?"

"Your majesty, it is good to see you again."

King Harold stepped forward and placed his hand on Garth's shoulder. "It's good to see you again—though it's not much better than the last time we were together."

"Aye, your majesty—at least you weren't part of this one."

"Come; King Fredric waits to see you. You must eat with us and tell us all you know. Ransom and Annabeth, come get off your horse and join us."

"I am afraid that is impossible, sire. Annabeth needs the attention of a physician immediately."

King Harold stepped forward, peering at her though the darkness.

Eliot spoke. "Raburn had her on the rack. I am afraid her right shoulder is dislocated, and there is a wound on her side."

"You are the one who turned the rack," said Garth coldly.

"Only because he told me to," Eliot defended. "I took no pleasure from it, but I had a job to do. If it meant fulfilling my job and saving one more life, I thought it worth it."

"You put Annabeth on the rack?" asked Prince Alfred, stepping forward, disbelief in his words.

"Yes," Eliot sighed with discontent over the fact.

"And you thought her life was worth it?"

"If it fulfilled the purpose that I was commissioned for, yes."

Eliot was on the ground, Prince Alfred standing over him, daring Eliot to stand up and face him.

"Hold on, Prince Alfred. Don't blame him. I am the one who gave him the order to do whatever it took." King Harold was holding onto the prince's right arm, which had knocked Eliot down with a resounding hook.

"But you didn't twist an innocent girl in the rack," spat out Alf.

Ransom had a half wish to join Prince Alfred and give his friend a good piece of his mind.

"Leave him, Alf," whispered Annabeth, her voice hoarse. "That is all over now."

"If you say so, Anna," sighed Prince Alf, turning and taking her hand.

The night was dark and clouded; Alf sought to pierce it and look into his old playmate's aching eyes.

Annabeth wearily pulled her eyes shut and leaned into Ransom, holding back a groan. The pain was still strong, but it had lost the overpowering numbness, leaving a dull roar that made her ache everywhere.

King Harold called two pages to his side. "Show

Ransom to the girls' tent, and you, fetch my physician. Bring him to her tent at once. Garth, would you care to join us or will you go with your daughter?"

"I'll go with my daughter and join you later, if that is all right with you, your majesty."

"Very good. Your highness?"

"I am going with Annabeth," he answered flatly, giving Eliot a look that could have killed him.

The page took the bridle and led them to a nearby tent. Christina's voice could be heard singing softly inside.

At the sound of the familiar voice, Annabeth opened her eyes to see Alf smiling.

"Christina!" called Alf, making their presence known.

A moment later, that maiden appeared, fresh and pretty with a new dress and a ribbon in her hair. "Yes, Alf, what did you…?" She stopped short at the sight of the others.

"Anna's here. Can she have the second cot?"

"Of course. Come on in. Anna, there are so many wonderful things I have to show you. What is the matter, Annabeth? You don't look well."

"She isn't," answered Prince Alfred. "Ransom, let me take her in," said the prince, turning to him.

"No. I don't want to jostle her more than I have to."

"It's all right, Ransom. I can take it," she whispered, but Ransom ignored her.

"Eliot, could you get that crate and put it beside the horse?"

In a moment, Ransom swung his leg over the neck of the horse, then gently slid onto the crate and stepped onto the ground. He carried her into the tent and lowered her delicately onto her cot.

Ransom had held her arm in a sling-like position against his body, and it felt strange to have her out of his arms; it was as if she was imprinted against him.

Her eyes met his, and a feeling rose in his chest, almost making it impossible to breathe.

"Thank you, Ransom." Annabeth whispered, almost closing her eyes to hide the pain he saw in them.

Leaning over her, he brushed away a stray piece of hair that had been plastered against her face.

Just then, her father was beside her and Annabeth shifted her gaze to him.

"There is my Annabeth."

"I haven't failed you, have I, Father?" she whispered, tears gathering in her eyes.

"You could never fail me."

Annabeth bit her lip to keep back the cry that swelled in her throat, making it feel hollow and dry.

"It's all right, Annabeth. There is no need to cry. It's all over. You've held out this long; you needn't shed a tear."

The desire to cry built in her chest with a crushing weight. She took in a deep breath and closed her eyes. Her father was right; there was no need to cry. No need—the worst of it was over. The pain in her chest eased.

A moment later, the physician entered and glanced at his patient. His face soured.

"I'll need help."

"I'll help," Garth offered before Ransom could speak.

The doctor looked him over. "At first I thought you were my patient, but then I saw her." He glanced at Ransom. "Since it is a young lady, will you enquire if the lady outside will come and help us?"

Ransom went to Lady Christina. She paled at the prospect, but nodded that she would and followed him back towards the tent. Ransom swept aside the tent flap for Christina to enter, but before he could set foot in the tent himself the physician turned to him.

"That will be all. I'll call if I need anything."

Reluctantly, he left and stood with Prince Alfred and Eliot. Someone had to keep those two from fighting--again.

In several minutes, there came a shuddering sound and a sharp outcry of pain from Annabeth. All of the men winced—even Eliot.

A quarter of an hour later, Christina came stumbling through the tent flap, her face white and body shaking. At the sight of Alf, she rushed forward, and he opened his arms to her. Sobs broke from her as she buried her face against his arm.

"Oh Alf, Alf! She did it for us. For us."

Ransom watched the prince whisper words of comfort in her ear and in a little while Lady Christina tried to compose herself.

Just then a servant came up. "Your highness, Eliot, and Garth are wanted at the kings' tent immediately."

For a moment Ransom wondered at the fact that his name wasn't mentioned and then was glad for it.

Christina slipped inside the tent to relay the

message to Garth, and in a moment, Annabeth's father departed.

Ransom stood anxiously at the entrance of the tent, wanting to come in but wondering if he dared with the snappish doctor waiting to be riled. Annabeth would need peace and quiet to recover.

He listened to the doctor giving orders to Christina about nursing Annabeth back to health. The girl sounded puzzled and flustered. He could sense her turning bright red.

The physician stepped out, calling back through the curtain. "I'll be back in an hour to check on her," then adding in a surprised voice as he nearly collided into Ransom, "What are you still doing here, sir? No matter." He stalked off, filled with his own self-importance.

A moment later, Christina was at the flap. "Oh, thank goodness it's you! He has left me to nurse Annabeth and I—"

Ransom didn't need to hear another word. He laid his hand on her shoulder. "I'll help if you wish."

He felt all of her anxiety leave beneath his touch.

"Oh, good. Come in please."

She started to relay all the doctor's orders word for word, but when it came to the assortment of powders and potions he had left for Annabeth to take, she became confused almost to the point of tears, and she began to wring her hands.

"Oh, I don't remember a thing he said now."

"I think I can figure it out well enough," supplied Ransom. Being a bounty hunter meant having to know some medical basics in order to heal and keep one's self well.

In a moment, Ransom sorted through the jumble and set everything right.

Now that disaster by Christina was averted, he turned his attention to Annabeth.

She was conscious—her face pale, her lips pressed tight to keep from crying. At the cool touch of his hand on her hot forehead, she opened her eyes.

The pain was back in full force. Her shoulder had been reset. The chains in the dungeon and the long ride there had upset it painfully.

Biting her lower lip was the best she could do to keep back a cry. Annabeth wanted to writhe, but that would only hurt worse, so she wiggled her toes instead.

"It hurts," she barely whispered to him, then wondered why she had. Even while they had been traveling, when he had bound her wound, she hadn't admitted it. Why now?

"I know." His eyes were soft with care. It was then that she realized it: he wanted to know. "I want you to take something that should help and make you sleepy. You need your rest."

Annabeth nodded her head with a wince, pressing her lips together.

In a few minutes, he placed his cool hand beneath her neck.

"Drink this, then close your eyes. If you want anything you need only ask."

Annabeth started to nod, then whimpered at the pulsating ache that tingled through every nerve of her body.

Something bitter passed her lips, but she was in too much pain to care what it tasted like.

Everything started to feel like it was burning around her, and she could not help her whimpers. Gradually she felt nothing, and fell asleep.

CHAPTER 21

Ransom turned over and opened his eyes. The soft morning sun made the white of his canvas tent look warm and yellow. A breeze came through the tent flap comfortably. He sank his shoulder into the cot.

"You like her, don't you?"

The sound of Eliot's voice suddenly made the world not so beautiful.

Of all people to share a tent with, why him? But Ransom turned over and glanced at Eliot, who was turning his dagger over and over in his hand mechanically, lost in thought.

"How is Annabeth?" Eliot asked.

"Why would you care?"

Eliot was silent.

Ransom decided to prod him. "Why *would* you care? You are the one who twisted her on the rack."

Eliot broke from his mute reverie. "I was only doing what I had to do to prove myself. A man isn't a man if he can lower himself to torturing a girl. Twisting it hard was the only way I knew how to get her off quickly—jerking, instead of one slow degree at a time for hours and hours. I wanted her to remain the same. Not…" He shuddered. "I didn't have another choice."

Eliot swung his legs over the edge of his cot and rubbed his jaw. "That prince has a mean punch."

"They've been friends since they were children."

"Hmm. Makes sense. Keep your eyes on her, Ransom. She is going to need you."

"What?" said Ransom, sitting upright. Something about Eliot's words startled him.

"She is going to need you."

"And *what* makes you say that?"

Eliot shrugged. "Gut feeling. Don't like it, but it's there all the same." He pulled on his doublet and left.

Ransom eased back into his cot. He hadn't realized until last night as he was closing his eyes that he hadn't slept in over a day. Weariness still pulled at him, but Eliot's words disturbed him. He had to go see Annabeth. Hopefully, it wasn't too early.

In s few minutes he was standing outside the girls' tent, asking for entrance. He was admitted by Lady Christina, who still looked anxious and flustered by her position as nurse.

"How is she doing?"

Christina shrugged one shoulder. "The physician said she is doing as well as can be expected, but she has that same pained look, and she is still so pale. I am worried, Ransom."

Ransom took a seat by the cot and touched Annabeth's hand. It was warm but not feverish. Her body was fighting, but not in a struggle that would take her life into dangerous territory.

At his touch, Annabeth's eyes fluttered open and she blinked several times.

"I am sorry. I didn't mean to wake you, Beth."

"It's all right. I think I was already awake. What is going on?"

Ransom smiled. "I am not really sure, and I am not really sure I care. I know they have plans to attack Raburn, but nothing more."

"Have you seen my father?"

"Not this morning."

Annabeth nodded. He could tell by the look in her eyes she was still very weary. He couldn't blame her. She had let go of her strength in the dungeon so everything would just slip away from her. Now she was ready and willing to fight for her life, but it would take time to recover.

But it was more than just that. After all of these months, she longed to have her father by her side—to see him, to be near him always—and Ransom couldn't blame her one bit. He would do anything to be with his family again, but that was never to be. They were gone, all gone. Ransom let his mind numb. He didn't want to think about that.

"Do you want me to go see if I can find him?"

"He'll come when he is able," whispered Annabeth, trying to hide the pain in her voice. "Maybe I will rest just a little bit more

Unexpectedly, Ransom found Annabeth slipping her hand into his, holding it loosely. He looked at her, his eyes asking questions.

Annabeth smiled, sighed, and closed her eyes.

Chapter 22

"Annabeth? Annabeth."

The voice made her pull her eyes open and turn on her cot. The pain ached through her shoulder and down her spine, but when she saw her father she smiled.

"Hello, Father."

"Hello, daughter. How are you?"

"Better…and you?" she asked trying to sound strong.

"Very well; very well indeed. They have their assault plans ready for Anondorf Castle. I just wish I was able to lead them. Nothing would give me as much pleasure as that."

"Won't it be dangerous, Father?"

"Anything worth fighting for has a tendency to be dangerous, my daughter. But you know that."

For a long time there was silence, neither knowing what to say. It had been so long.

"How are you feeling?"

"Better. I missed you."

"I missed you too. Every day I prayed for your

safety."

"And every day I prayed for yours."

There was another long silence, and slowly Annabeth raised her eyes to meet his, trying to keep back the tears.

"I am sorry for getting you into this mess. If I hadn't told you, nothing like this would have happened."

"Annabeth. I am glad you told me. I trusted him, and he betrayed us. I knew what it would cost. I never thought that you would fight for me; I thought you would flee and hide like any other daughter in the kingdom would have. I never dreamed that you would champion a cause."

"Did you mind that, Father?"

"Not one bit."

"What are we going to do now?"

"Now?"

"Now that you no longer work for Lord Raburn, what are we going to do?"

"Don't know; haven't really thought that far." He laughed. "I never thought I would make it out of Raburn's dungeon alive."

Annabeth tightened her hand around her father's. "I was so scared of losing you."

He smiled. "You needn't fear losing me ever, Annabeth. I will love you no matter where you are." He leaned forward and kissed her forehead. "I love you, my Annabeth."

"I love you, Father."

The next moment Annabeth felt her father shudder in pain. His body trembled, and he turned pale.

"Father? Father, what is it?" she asked, sitting up, ignoring the vivid pain that shot through her body .

Then she saw *him,* and her heart stopped. The words fell from her lips in horror and unbelief.

"Lord Raburn, what are you doing here?"

The man only smiled. "Your rescuers blazed a trail here, and now you will all pay." He raised a dagger and plunged it towards her. Annabeth, was frozen in shock and horror. The only thing that she could use was her voice. Opening her mouth, she screamed. It seemed to break the terror inside of her loose, as the blade descended towards her heart, she tumbled from her cot.

The knife ripped into the fabric and struck into the ground.

Annabeth tried to scramble to her feet to find something to defend herself with, but he was standing on her dress, making escape impossible. She searched for something—anything within reach. Then Annabeth's eyes fell on the dagger thrust into her father's back.

The world stopped.

Nothing mattered.

It was all a blur frozen in time that would never stop. There were no sounds, nothing—nothing but the screaming silence.

The hands of King Harold were turning over her father. His still-conscious eyes broke her frozen world. His lips were mouthing her name. In a moment, she had pillowed his head on her lap and was soothing his pained brow with her good hand.

"Annabeth," his voice strained with the word, and his breathing came with perilous labor.

"I am here, Father. I am here!"

His pain-blurred eyes cleared and he looked into her face, smiling as he did so.

"You have made me so proud, Annabeth. I am honored to call you my daughter."

She slipped her hand into his and held it tightly; his grip growing weaker.

Unexpectedly, Annabeth found herself surrounded.

Her father's eyes strayed to those around them.

"Please take care of my daughter," he whispered.

"I will."

"She shall want for nothing."

Annabeth looked up and saw both kings kneeling by her father's side. She looked back at her father. His eyes were closing. Suddenly they opened and looked up at her.

"Don't leave me, Father. Please don't," she begged. Tears were running down her face. She pressed his cold hand against her cheek.

"I can't help it, my strong one, my lovely, my daughter—I am going." He struggled for breath, and pressed his hand against her cheek. "I love you, Annabeth." A fleeting smile passed his lips, and his hand dropped to his side.

"No..." Annabeth whispered, her voice barely passing her throat, swollen with tears. "Oh, Father, no. Don't leave me." She laid her head against his strong chest and let grief swallow her.

How many hands Annabeth had pushed away, she didn't know. Nor did she care. She wanted to stay with her father. Her heart had been shattered into tiny pieces, and each throbbed in her chest like a shard of glass, making it almost impossible for her to breathe—

to *want* to breathe.

Then there was the quiet touch that came not to take her away from her father, but to share her grief. His hand ran gently, almost imperceptibly, across her burning shoulders.

"Beth," Ransom whispered, gently piercing the silence with his quiet voice. "It's all over. Raburn is dead; his army has surrendered. Your war is won, Annabeth."

Slowly, she raised her eyes to meet his.

"But I lost the most important thing. I couldn't protect him. I—I— Ransom!" She buried her head against his shoulder, sobs shaking her.

In a moment, Ransom had gathered her up in his arms and held her close to his heart.

"Annabeth, he died protecting you, his daughter, the person he loved most on this earth. You can't protect everyone, Annabeth. Sometimes you can't even protect yourself. It's what makes you human; it's what makes people fall in love with you. Annabeth, no one is perfect." He lifted her face to look into his. "We can't be perfect, Annabeth."

"But if I had just…"

He laid his finger on her lips. "No. You are tired and worn out—you need your rest."

"I've rested too long. If I hadn't been, maybe it wouldn't have happened. Maybe..."

Ransom pressed his finger against her mouth again. With a resigned sigh, Annabeth laid her head against his shoulder, her body heaving with grief.

In a minute, Ransom was holding a pewter goblet to her mouth and telling her to drink it.

"I don't want anything."

"Just take a little. You need to restore your strength."

With great reluctance, Annabeth sipped the bitter liquid, then buried her face in Ransom's leather jerkin, clinging to him with desperation. The world grew black at the edges, and slowly crept towards her. Weariness stalked her body. She wanted to fight it off, but found it impossible. Ransom's arms were strong. They would protect her; she trusted him.

CHAPTER 23

Ransom had been reluctant to follow his king's orders to sedate Annabeth. But when he had seen and heard her for himself, he knew she needed rest or she would exhaust herself.

He watched as Annabeth went limp in his arms, completely trusting, worn out body, heart, and soul. She almost looked dead, save for the twinge of pink in her cheeks. Ransom winced as his mind flashed over what had happened, and he pulled her close. Ransom bowed his head over Annabeth's, pressing a kiss into her hair. He brushed away the stray loose hairs that fell about her face and gathered her into his arms.

She had almost died, in fact, just as he had entered the tent only a few moments after her terrified scream.

That scream.

He shivered.

Seeing her on the ground terrified, paralyzed with grief, and that knife hanging over her head…He had almost killed Lord Raburn on sight, but had refrained himself. In a moment Eliot was there and only as Eliot could, he fished the plans out of the man…the army hiding in the woods, ready to attack.

They hadn't needed to talk; they knew each other's minds from training, and in an instant charged into action.

The two of them had gotten Raburn's small army to surrender. Most of the men had been tired of Raburn's tyranny, but had been too afraid to do anything against his will.

Prince Alfred had found him and asked him to come. Ransom had, and now she was in his arms, unconscious. Men were watching him as he carried Annabeth to her new quarters.

Annabeth was a legend in so many minds. She was just a girl in his—one who needed protection and love like any other girl, except she needed it more, because people didn't see her that way. She didn't want to disappoint them, so she struggled onward, hiding her pain, her suffering—trying to be everything they needed and everything she needed. It would break her if she didn't stop.

Ransom laid Annabeth on her new cot, pulling blankets over her. He stood there wondering, worried. Just then, Lady Christina came in.

"Is she going to make it?"

Ransom shrugged and shook his head; he didn't

know. For his own heart's sake, he wished she would. But for her? Could she really live through another tragedy in her life? It had been struck with grief and pain so many times, slashing her heart to pieces. Her heart had healed together again, but this was different.

Oh, God, do what is best for Annabeth. Keep her safe from more harm, fill her with Your love. Amen.

Ransom smiled softly. Annabeth was right. Everything would be beautiful in His time. Whatever that was, wherever it happened, He would make things beautiful.

Silently, Ransom slipped out of the tent. King Harold said that he wanted Ransom's presence in his tent after Annabeth had been comfortably settled.

"Your majesty," he greeted with a bow as he was ushered into the joint meeting tent.

"How is Annabeth?" asked King Harold.

"Sleeping, at least for now."

"Good. Now, we have some business to discuss. You have done much for Beltarra, and King Fredric would like to honor you. He would like to knight you and give you lands of your own; however, he realizes this might not be agreeable to your lifestyle, and in that case there is a large reward of money waiting for you."

"And what do you think, your majesty? Should I

accept?"

"You are free to do as you wish, Ransom—when have you ever done anything else?"

Ransom bowed his head with a slight smile. "Please tell King Fredric that I thank him very warmly for the offers, and I would be delighted to accept one, but would like for some time to consider."

"What—you can't decide on the spot? Ransom, my man who always knows exactly what he wants, can't make up his mind?"

"It is not just my own feelings that I wish to consult."

"Ah, is that the way the wind blows," said King Harold, not trying to hide his smile. "I never thought you would settle down."

Ransom ignored his king's comment.

King Harold sighed reluctantly. "Well, that complicates matters slightly with Annabeth. Not that they weren't complicated already."

"What are your plans for her?" asked Ransom.

"Her father charged both of us with Annabeth's care, but since he didn't leave her in either of our charge but rather collectively, we have been trying to decide what to do for her. Naturally, King Fredric would like to keep her as one of his subjects—she was practically raised in his court, though she was never a courtier. And I feel more than an obligation to her. Her father saved my life, and I want to do what is best by her. So it has been decided that whomever she decides to go with, she shall be their ward and the other will provide her with a dowry. We would both like to make her a lady, as well, but that is something Annabeth would have to want. She has been raised around the titled all of her life, and she's never shown much of an inclination on that subject. But then again, things might have changed. Her father should have been a knight—he deserved the title."

Ransom wondered if Annabeth's head would spin at such prospects.

Anxiously Ransom counted the days before the physician thought her body was strong enough to bear the shock of what had happened. When it came at last, it was thought best that he should be the one beside her. She had fallen asleep in his arms; she should wake with him at hand.

Quietly, Ransom sat beside the bed, trying not to feel fidgety and anxious. Slowly Annabeth's eyes opened, and she looked around the tent.

"How are you feeling, Annabeth?"

"Better; thank you," she said, reaching out and

taking his hand. "Was it all real or was it just a dream?"

"I wish I could tell you it was just a dream." He sighed.

"My father…is he really gone?" There was a choke in her voice.

Ransom nodded. "Lord Raburn is dead. His army surrendered the moment they saw his cause was a lost one."

Annabeth sighed and looked up at the tent's slanted ceiling.

"I am sorry, Annabeth."

"Sorry, for what? You didn't do anything to hurt me."

Ransom raised her hand and kissed it gently before looking her in the eye. "I am sorry I couldn't do more."

Annabeth looked at him. "You've done more than enough. You have done more than I could."

"What on earth makes you say that?"

Tears swelled in Annabeth's eyes, and she turned away.

"What is it, Annabeth?"

"I don't know how to face it. I don't know…how to bear this. My father was the last thing I had, and now—it's all gone." There was a gasp of pain and held back sobs that came from deep within. She bit her dry lower lip to keep back the tears.

"Do you remember when you told me that God makes all things beautiful in His time?"

"Don't throw my words back in my face, please," she whispered, her voice choked with the tears trying to burst in her throat.

"Beth. I don't want to hurt you, but you are right. He does make everything beautiful."

Annabeth turned further away, trying not to shake with crying, struggling to be strong, to be fine, to just survive with her shattered heart.

"When I was twelve, our village was raided by a northern country. I was out fishing with a friend. By the time we got back our entire village was devastated. Gone. Every parent, brother, sister. The raiders attacked me and my friend. I was too scared to fight back. I fled; he stood his ground and was murdered where he stood, defenseless. That day that I determined that I would never run from a fight, that I would never be unarmed or unable to help those around me. I would learn to master weapons, and I would destroy whoever dared to cross the law. For years, I studied and trained with a traveling swordsman. I learned everything I could from him and eventually could even master my master and any swordsman I came across. Then the king came across me at one of his tournaments and hired me for all kinds of different jobs.

"I was taught from boyhood that God has a purpose for everything that happens in a life. I never could understand why He took my family, my four brothers and sisters; why did He take what I loved most out my life? Why? Now I understand. Annabeth, He has given me the heart of a warrior, a defender, a protector. If that hadn't happened when I was boy, Annabeth, I wouldn't have been here. I wouldn't be the man I am today, as much as I ache still for my family. All of the things I have done in my life—I don't regret any of them. Annabeth, I wouldn't change a thing. He has made my life beautiful, He has given it purpose where I could see none. He will give you purpose; He will give you beauty…"

Annabeth started to cry, her body shaking with heartbroken pain.

Ransom gathered her up in his arms and held her close. Annabeth shivered under his hand and pressed her head against his shoulder, crying. She shook, holding her breath, making the tears stop, and gripping her sorrows firmly.

"Oh, Ransom, if I could have faith like that."

He gently pulled her away, catching her chin in his hand, then tilted her face upward to meet his gaze.

"You have it, Beth; it just seems so dark you can't see it. He is there; He will make things beautiful. You will see in time. It will heal. You will carry a scar in your heart for your father all of your life, but it will make you better than you ever were."

She looked at him helpless, afraid, wounded. "Tell me it will be all right," Annabeth whispered.

Ransom pulled her close, slipping an arm around her and smoothing her hair with his hand.

Annabeth held onto his doublet with tight fists, as if holding on for dear life.

"You'll be all right," he whispered. "Someday, sooner or later, it will all make sense. Everything will be beautiful for you, too."

CHAPTER 24

Annabeth retired to her tent, her head reeling. She sank down on her cot, placed her head in her hands, and rubbed her temples.

What do I do? Oh, God, what should I do? She had never thought beyond day by day, sometimes hour by hour; at times her survival depended upon mere seconds. Now, unexpectedly, her life stood long before her, full—full of questions, questions she had no idea how to answer.

Annabeth had just spoken with King Fredric and then with King Harold. Their plans for her were incredible, and she felt overwhelmed, honored, and unworthy.

"Annabeth?" It was Song Lark's voice at the flap of her tent.

"Come in," she invited. "How are you, Song Lark?"

"Much better than you are, I think," he answered, strumming the strings of his lute.

"I have a feeling you're right. I haven't the faintest clue of what I should do."

Song Lark chuckled and patted her cheek affectionately. "You'll figure it out. But I have come to say my farewell."

"You're leaving?" Annabeth exclaimed in dismay. "You can't leave; not yet."

"I don't dare stay any longer. My lute is longing to be played, and my feet are itching to be on the road."

"I half wish I could go with you."

"Why would you want to do a thing like that?"

Annabeth sighed and sagged back onto her cot. "I am tired. I want—I want… I don't know what I want."

"You want to get away from everything you've known, is that it? But to get away from everything you have ever known seems disloyal and untrue, and so unlike yourself, you don't know what to do."

"But I don't want to leave forever. I just—" Annabeth sighed.

"You'll figure it out, Annabeth," he said, patting her head. "But for now, farewell!" Strumming the strings of his lute, he made a cadenced step out of the tent, singing with all of his heart.

I once knew a maid
Who carried a blade
Oh hey nonie nonie na no.
I once knew a man
Who had no plan
Oh hey nonie nonie na no.
Together they fought

And a victory wrought
Oh hey nonie nonie na no.

...

And Song Lark and his verses were gone.

Annabeth walked to the far side of her tent. She mustn't run. She had gotten so used to running it almost felt a part of her, but then again, it wasn't what she wanted.

What did she really, truly want? It came to her mind, but she shoved it aside as impossible. Ransom's face had flashed before her in her mind's eye. It wasn't really possible. She turned around, only to start in surprise.

"Oh, hello, Eliot. Can I do something for you?"

"Sorry. I didn't mean to frighten you."

"You didn't frighten me. I was just startled, that's all."

Eliot's mouth twisted into a smile. "Of course. I called out twice, but when I didn't get an answer I thought I would come in."

"I am sorry; my mind was elsewhere."

"You needn't apologize. It is I who has come to apologize."

"For what?"

"Can you really be so forgiving to a man who captured you and put you on the rack? Not only that, but turned it and did this?" he said, touching her shoulder.

"You were only doing what you thought you had to. It was your job. You had to make him believe you. If you hadn't, I still might be down there and had it been anyone else I would most likely dead."

"I don't know about that. I have never seen a girl fight like you have."

"I gave up down there. I wouldn't have made it out without..." She let her words trail off into silence.

"Ransom is a good man. We trained together when the king hired us for his service. There are few men I admire more than him."

She nodded in agreement, still feeling silent and puzzled by what she was struggling with in the back of her mind.

"Annabeth. I am sorry for what I did; I truly regret it. Please, forgive me."

"I already have. You are forgiven," she said, offering him her hand.

He took it with a smile tweaking the corners of his mouth. "It has been an honor to know you, and I hope that if you decide to become my king's ward that I will see you often."

"Did he make you come here to try to convince me?"

Eliot's eyes smiled quietly. "No. I just wanted to make sure I would not be a roadblock in your decision making. Your choices are difficult ones."

"Yes, they are. Thank you for coming. I appreciate it."

"It was my privilege and honor."

Just then, Prince Alfred came bursting through the tent door. "Annabeth!" He stopped short on seeing Eliot. His posture bristled.

"What are you doing here?" accused Prince Alfred, his eyes sparking with slowly warming anger.

"Is it customary for you to come bursting into a young lady's tent like that?"

"What right have you to correct me?"

"And what right have you to come barging in here?"

"That is none of your business. I demand an apology. No, on second thought, I think you should apologize to Annabeth for all you have put her through." Prince Alfred growled.

"Alfred, please."

"Annabeth, do you have any idea who this man is?"

"I am not so daft in my head that I do not know the man who played my captor."

"He did more than play it, Anna. This man hurt

you."

"I am perfectly aware of that, your highness. Please, Alf, stop."

"Annabeth!"

"She asked you to stop, your highness. Why don't you honor her wishes?" interrupted Eliot.

"You stay out of this. It concerns Anna and me—not you."

"I am afraid it does. I am standing here, and the conversation is about me."

Prince Alfred glared at him dangerously.

"Alf, please, let it be for now. What did you want to see me about?"

"I came to see if you had made up your mind yet."

Annabeth sighed and let her shoulders sag. "I haven't. Not yet."

"Well, I am just letting you know there is a place for you always in Lady Christina's and my court."

"You and Christina?"

"Yes. Our court," he said with a smile. "Father finalized that while you were ill. We spent so much time together that…we fell in love."

Annabeth suddenly felt baffled beyond anything she had ever felt. "Congratulations," she managed at last. "I wish you the greatest joy in all the world. You deserve it."

"Thank you, Annabeth. Now do say yes and add to our joy. Please. Christina and I have talked it over, and she desperately wants you to be one of her ladies in waiting."

"I don't know, Alfred. I will really have to think about it, and I am feeling very tired right now, so if you don't mind…"

"Of course. Think about it as long as you need to."

"I will."

"Thank you, Annabeth."

"Aren't you going to apologize for just bursting in here?" asked Eliot, his arms folded over his chest, his eyes challenging the prince.

"Annabeth is a friend of mine. I have committed no crime, and I certainly don't intend to take advice from a man such as yourself. If you ask me, Anna shouldn't even consider any sort of proposal from a country that can hurt her like that. Your king and your country put her life in jeopardy"

"Alfred, they also rescued me. Besides, my father and King Harold became good friends. Please don't speak of it."

"Fine. I won't, but I still think this man has much to answer for."

"He has apologized, your highness. Now please leave off quarreling. It is all over and done with."

"All right, if that is what you really want…but I still think that…"

"My king has nothing to do with this mess. My orders came directly from *your* father, Prince Alfred. He told me do whatever needed to be done. He gave me the orders to help Raburn find Annabeth and bring her in."

"My father would never do any such thing!"

"Your father has just come from a battlefield where he has seen worse things happen."

"My father would never give such an order."

"Then ask him yourself."

"Tell me why your king said he gave the order."

"He knew you wouldn't understand your father."

"You are a liar!"

"Prove it."

Prince Alf swung his right fist towards Eliot, who ducked, landing a direct blow into the prince's stomach. For a moment Alfred doubled over in pain, but a second later the prince's angry fists were firing at Eliot again. Faking another right hook, he caught Eliot firmly in the jaw with his left. Eliot saved himself from a complete fall and was up again in a moment. With a swing of his fists, he caught Prince Alfred on the side of his face.

After the first few moments of shock wore off,

Annabeth began to protest. "Stop it. Alfred! Eliot. Stop! Stop it, please."

At that moment, Ransom entered.

"What on earth is going on here?"

Neither of the men answered, and Annabeth was too distressed to respond.

Grabbing the back of Eliot's jerkin, Ransom pulled then pushed him out of the tent. As Prince Alfred went after him, Ransom caught him and walked towards the back of the tent.

"Stop it!" protested Prince Alfred, trying to shake off Ransom's strong, coolheaded arms.

"No, you stop it."

A moment later, Eliot came rushing back in.

Annabeth grabbed onto Eliot's arm. At her touch he stopped, breathing heavily.

"I'll tear you to pieces," muttered Alf through clenched teeth; he was still boiling with anger. "How dare you accuse my father of such an action!"

Eliot's anger had calmed.

"Because it's true."

"Eliot. Stop this," commanded Ransom; his voice was calm, but anger hid in his firm tone.

"I am not the one who started it."

Ransom sent him an angry look, then turned to Prince Alfred.

"What were you thinking? You should know better, especially with Annabeth in her weak condition. She has been through enough without the two of you coming in here and fighting like street urchins who don't know any better."

"You are right. I shall call for a truce. No more angry words between us; at least not in Annabeth's presence. We shall settle it like true gentlemen and get to the bottom of this matter."

"Agreed," answered Eliot.

"I am going to go see my father," said Alf, brushing by Eliot. At the tent door, Alf turned back and looked at Annabeth. "I am sorry, Anna."

"It's all right, Alf."

In a moment, Eliot and Prince Alfred were gone.

"Are you all right, Beth?"

"I am fine," her voice was sharp.

"What is the matter?" Ransom asked, turning Annabeth to face him.

"I can take care of myself, Ransom. Thank you for your help. You may go if you wish," she said, pushing his hands away.

Ransom waited a moment, wanting to look into Annabeth's eyes, but they refused to meet his.

"Well, I better make sure those two don't kill each other. I'll see you later, Annabeth."

"Yes, that would be a good idea."

Slowly, Ransom walked past her and to the tent entrance. Annabeth spun around.

"Ransom."

He paused and turned back slightly.

"Yes?"

"Of all the people I could be angry with, it shouldn't be you. I am sorry. I shouldn't have spoken so harshly. I was wrong. Forgive me, please?"

"Of course I forgive you, Annabeth," he said, and started to leave.

"Ransom."

"Yes?"

Annabeth bit her lip before she dared let the question pass her lips. "Do you really think I am weak?"

In two steps he was by her side. Taking her face in his hands, he lifted it to meet his own. "No, I don't think you are weak. You are one of the strongest people I have ever known. Is that what hurt you—why you spoke sharply to me?"

"Yes. I am sorry it was so petty. But I need to be strong right now. There is so much to decide, and my head gets so dizzy. I—I don't know what to do, Ransom, and when you said that, my silly pride rose and snapped. I am so sorry…"

Ransom laid his finger over her mouth. "Shh. It's

all right."

Annabeth met his eyes. Something in her pulled to lean against him, to let herself cry on his shoulder. But she bit her lip and took a deep breath instead.

"So they told you all of their grand plans for you?" Ransom asked.

"Yes, and I haven't a clue what I should do. They told me to do what I want, but I really don't know what I want. I have been working all of this time to get my father free and I was going to do whatever he wanted—and he didn't even have plans. He didn't think he'd get out of Raburn's prison." Annabeth took a deep breath and let it out. Her head was spinning again, and she wrung her hands, trying to get her nerves to stop flying about in her chest like restless butterflies.

Ransom caught Annabeth's anxious hands. Her palms were sweaty. "What do you want?"

"That is the thing; I don't know."

"No. I am asking what do *you* want?"

Annabeth looked up at him, confused.

Ransom stepped closer, looking into her eyes.

"Forget everything they have offered you, everything that anyone has ever asked you. Forget about trying to please the King Harold or King Fredric or Alf or anyone else. What do you want to see happen in your life?"

"I—" she shook her head, her brow wrinkling with confusion.

"Close your eyes."

With a resigned sigh, Annabeth obeyed.

Ransom whispered in her ear. "Now tell me what you wish for most of all."

She shook her head.

"Do you want to go on being the mysterious Annabeth, carrying a sword all around the country, or would you like to become a great lady?"

"No." Annabeth shook her head and opened her eyes. "I just want to be me. I don't want riches; I don't want to have to fight. I will fight for what I love, but I don't want to have to fight all of my life. I don't much care what I do or where I go; I just want to love and be loved. I have dreamed of living in a cottage by a laughing stream, and having children, and…" Annabeth stopped short and shook her head. "I am such a foolish dreamer. I am sorry." She started to turn away, her heart beating frantically in her chest. She had said much more than she had planned on saying to anyone, ever.

Ransom caught her hands.

"Can I share one of my dreams with you?"

Annabeth looked up at Ransom, puzzled. "What?"

"You see, I have a dream. It is about sharing a

cottage by a stream with the woman I love. And I love her not because she is amazing with a sword, or because she is strong, or because she is a hero and the beginning of a legend. I love her because she has a tender heart, a gentle hand, an inward beauty that steals my heart. I want to protect, love, cherish, and always be with her." Ransom stopped and swallowed the lump in his throat.

Annabeth was looking at him as one transfixed.

"That is my dream, Annabeth, and I would be honored if you would share it with me."

"Are you in earnest?"

"I would not have spoken if it wasn't with an earnest heart—one that is all yours, if you want it."

"That is what I want most of all."

"Will you marry me, Annabeth?" he asked, stepping close and slipping his arms around her.

"Yes, Ransom. With all my heart, yes."

THE END

ABOUT THE AUTHOR

Jessica Greyson fell in love with words through the worlds crafted in classic novels that forged heroic characters. At age twelve she felt the calling to be His ready writer and took up her pen to start crafting characters and worlds of her own; finally publishing her first novel ten years later. While traipsing the world, teaching, reading, and learning to love the people that her King created, she has carefully carved out time to remain an avid writer. You can learn more about the adventures of Jessica Greyson & her characters at jessicagreyson.com

ABOUT THE ARTIST

Louie Roybal attended Pensacola Christian College. He majored in Commercial Art and Graphic Design. He has a love for both and desires to produce fine art at a casual rate while working in the graphic design industry.

Louie currently works full time as a graphic designer, and free-lances to selected clients on the side.

You can see more of his work at louieroybal.com

www.ingramcontent.com/pod-product-compliance
Lightning Source LLC
Chambersburg PA
CBHW020912310726
48980CB00011B/847/J

* 9 7 8 0 9 8 8 4 6 1 4 6 8 *